A WYATT
BOOK *for*

W

— ST. —
MARTIN'S
PRESS

Claudia Casper

THE
RECONSTRUCTION

A Wyatt Book *for* St. Martin's Press
New York

Library of Congress Cataloging-in-Publication Data

Casper, Claudia.
    The reconstruction / Claudia Casper.
        p.   cm.
    "A Wyatt Book for St. Martin's Press."
    ISBN 0-312-18164-7
    1. Australopithecus afarensis—Fiction.   2. Fossil man—Africa—Fiction.   I. title.
PR9199.3.C4315R43   1997
813'.54—dc20   96-29245
                                                                 CIP

First published in Canada by the Penguin Group

First A Wyatt Book *for* St. Martin's Press Paperback
Edition: March 1998

10   9   8   7   6   5   4   3   2   1

For my early mentors
Helen Patterson
and
Greta Greisman
may their memories always be blessed

The process of reconstruction is like
a dissection in reverse.

—*John Gurche*

If little penis worms ruled the sea
I have no confidence that
Australopithecus would ever have
walked erect on the savannas
of Africa.

—*Stephen Jay Gould*
Wonderful Life

Acknowledgments

I would like to thank my husband and first reader James Griffin. This book would not have been possible without him. I owe a large debt to scientific artist, John Gurche, for his generosity with his time and his vast knowledge of hominid reconstructions. Thanks to: Larry O'Reilly, Chief of Exhibits at the Museum of Natural History, Washington DC; Bill Jungers, Professor of Anatomical Sciences at the State University of New York at Stonybrook; my charming dentist, Pierre Vigneault; artist David Dorrington; and my editor, Meg Masters, for her fine editorial touch. I'd also like to thank my parents, Mary Lou and Don Miller and Gordon Casper, and my friends, Marilou Appleby, Nora Blanck, Barb Hart, Steve Osborne and Maureen Moore.

A special thanks to Howard White, winner of the 1991 Stephen Leacock Award, writer, poet and publisher extraordinaire, for his undogmatic, essential advice.

The author also gratefully acknowledges the receipt of a Canada Council Explorations Grant that helped in the research and writing of this book.

THE
RECONSTRUCTION

ONE

"Wider please."

Her jaw ached but she obeyed, stretching her lips back further. She blinked up at his face. *I could bite your fingers off.* His eyes were a blurred blue concentration behind the saliva-spattered lenses of his glasses.

Margaret imagined what he saw. A tiny, detailed, oral world: particles of food being broken down by saliva; coffee stains near the gum line; fillings and caps and root canals that gave her a dental history unique enough to identify her body should she be disfigured in death. The inflamed slippery tissue of the tender pink gums and a floppy velvet tongue trying spasmodically not to get in the way, not to lay itself protectively over the areas he probed. Everything wet and glistening and red and imperfect. When he prodded with the curette she could smell the foul little odours that sometimes escaped.

The decay.

She wondered if dentists still enjoyed kissing. Did they still want to slip their tongues into a lover's mouth and explore the wet soft private place, did they still want to wind tongues sinuously like two snakes trying to penetrate each other's skins? Could dentists repress their daily observations of oral decay when it came to sex?

To kissing?

A narrow room with a low ceiling. The blue shadows of fir branches and lace curtains moving on the wall, a man's breath, his tongue moving supplely inside her mouth, his skin hot and surprisingly smooth against hers.

That night no longer seemed real. It seemed implausible that those lips had touched the body sitting now in the dentist's chair, or that her fingertips had pressed on his skin, that those moments—finite, discrete—existed objectively in her past. It seemed implausible that that night was not a dream. She didn't know his last name or address. She knew only that his first name was Phillip.

"You can close now."

Dr. Adin walked over to his cabinet and held an x-ray of her lower right jaw up to the light. He selected several tools from a cabinet drawer and they clinked metallically as he dropped them onto his stainless-steel tray. The throbbing pain had subsided as soon as she entered the front door of his office, as though the tooth sensed it was now in good hands.

Margaret looked out the window. A silver-haired woman waited at a bus stop across the street. The woman stared vacantly into the road and took no notice of people joining her at the stop.

Margaret remembered her childhood dentist's office,

which looked out over a cemetery. Her wisdom teeth hadn't erupted yet but all her adult teeth were in. It was summer and the window was open. She heard chickadees chirping and bluejays screeching and children calling to each other on the way home from school. The dentist pencilled notes on her chart.

"Well young lady," he said presently, "you have a cavity."

"But I thought you couldn't get cavities in your permanent teeth," she'd cried. "Aren't they supposed to last the rest of your life?"

"Only if you take very good care of them," he replied sternly.

She'd felt panicky. If she failed to brush her teeth, they might decay before she grew up. She was barely a teenager and decay had already taken root in her body.

Dr. Adin adjusted his hygienic mask. "Open please," he said through the white cotton.

Using a clamp carrier he picked up a metal clamp from the tray and jostled it over her molar, then released it. The clamp gripped the tooth, then slipped down slightly onto her gums so the serrated metal clamped the soft tissue. She winced.

She remembered her adolescent face, blurred by hormones, in the bathroom mirror. A heaviness had come over her, a kind of depression or passivity. She felt too heavy to run or jump. Often she felt too exhausted to brush her teeth. She'd go to bed, too weary even to take off her clothes, and curl up and quickly sink into unconsciousness. The next day she'd go to school wearing the clothes she'd slept in.

Weeks would go by. A sense of doom would build,

and then one day she'd be horrified by what she was doing. She'd rush to the bathroom mirror to examine her teeth, expecting rotten brown stumps, yet miraculously they'd gleam back at her, still white and even. And she would turn over a new leaf for a while, brushing and flossing three times a day.

People were always surprised when she said she had bad teeth. "They're so white and even, they're so beautiful. You have a lovely smile."

"They're full of cavities," she'd answer.

Dr. Adin snipped a small hole in the middle of a black latex dam. He stretched this opening over her tooth and pushed down, driving the edge of the clamp further into her gums. She gasped and gripped the chair's arms. Then he took some dental floss and forced the latex down between her teeth. She moaned.

"Did that hurt, Margaret?"

She took a deep breath. Relax. Soon this moment will be over. She nodded.

The dentist's assistant sprayed air on the frozen tooth. It felt like a cold electric shock.

Where pain is involved, waiting begins.

Margaret recrossed her ankles with the left foot on top, trying to divert her attention from her mouth. She looked out the window again at the woman standing at the bus stop, staring down at the asphalt. An expression of anguish suddenly passed over the woman's face, after which she seemed to become self-conscious and glanced round nervously to see if anyone watched her.

Pain changes time. You wait always for the present to end. The bus arrived and occluded Margaret's view of the stop. Hope lies in the quick termination of minutes.

You can spend your whole life just waiting for the next moment to be over.

The drill bit contacted her enamel and an unpleasant burning smell filled the room. Then he shone a light into her mouth. Time waiting for its own extinction. Her life was permeated by a kind of continuous background hum of low-grade emotional pain. She wasn't aware of it really, except that she remembered feeling differently as a child. Puberty had been like a disease for her. A disease she'd never really recovered from.

The drill whined like a giant mosquito. It turned decayed enamel into dust and made way for itself to move deeper.

The bus pulled away and the bus stop was deserted. She blamed Jane Goodall. That weekend she'd been reading a chapter on the sexual behaviour of the chimpanzees at Gombe Stream. The boisterous mating scene around a female in estrus, all the males converging on her pink, swollen bottom, restlessly lining up, had filled Margaret with envy. When she'd realized she was envious—she'd put the book down and wept.

Her sexual isolation inside her marriage seemed absolute. The quick thrust of a male chimp seeking to reproduce his genes seemed a level of pure sexual desire she herself could never hope to attract. She felt like a tree whose fruit was rotting on the branch.

John had stood by the front door, garment bag in hand, his face affecting the same wooden expressionlessness as her own, his voice intoning the same leaden bitterness. An hour after he'd left, her tooth began to throb; the pain clung to her all weekend long like sinew to a meat bone.

After packing the hole in her tooth with amalgam, Dr. Adin removed the latex dam and the clamp. His assistant vacuumed around her molar, causing more sensitivity shivers. The nozzle sought blood, pulp, shards of enamel among the saliva.

He held a carbon paper between her upper and lower teeth. "Bite... Grind... Open."

Her mother's voice, *Close your mouth. You'll catch a fly.* Margaret glanced at the office window. Open, but screened. In the garden sometimes, in the evening when Margaret kneeled down to pull up weeds, her lips would part slightly with effort and tiny flies did occasionally dart inside her mouth. What attracted them? The warm breathy darkness? Were they overcome by tiny impulses to self-destruct?

Her mother never seemed actually concerned about a fly really entering Margaret's mouth, nor did she seem concerned that her daughter might look moronic sitting slack-jawed and staring. It was more as though she was just mouthing something her own mother had said to her, a warning she'd never really understood the point of but repeated in the vacuum of any genuine maternal concerns of her own. Her mother had vaguely gone through the motions of motherhood, imitating what she imagined a good mother should be.

"You can close. We're done for today. It looks like we'll be seeing lots of each other this summer," Dr. Adin concluded cheerfully, as though he thought she might welcome this news.

"There are eight more cavities that I can see without x-rays. In six the decay has probably penetrated to the root system. Two are wisdom teeth, so they can be extracted. The other four will need root canals, and it's unlikely enough healthy enamel is left to do fillings. You'll need caps." He looked down at her chart. "You also have two smaller cavities but they can wait. We'll just keep an eye on them… You're on a dental plan?"

She shook her head. His cheerfulness changed to concern. "Mmmm. A root canal and cap run around $900, $1,000. The extractions will be around $200 each. The smaller fillings probably $180. In total you're looking in the neighbourhood of $5,000."

"I can't afford that right now." She took a deep breath, trying to quell tears. "What if I have the rotten ones pulled?"

"You can't do that," he said sternly. "The other teeth need support. You'd have to wear bridges and they're expensive too."

"What if I have them *all* pulled?" she asked. An end to decay. Perfect, white dentures. "How much would that cost?"

The dentist looked down at her in horror. "You're too young! No, I wouldn't advise that. You have such a pretty smile! I'd refuse to do it!"

She looked away. Her throat tightened and tears started again. She envisioned her face without the structural support of real teeth, the flesh around her mouth sagging and puckered, the jawbone weakening. She imagined a floppy gummy smile—defenceless and pathetic.

"Extraordinary stress can cause this kind of sudden decay," he said kindly, perhaps inquisitively. "It weakens the enamel." His white hair rose in unruly wisps like towering clouds on a windy spring day. His cheekbones were high and Slavic. The image of her toothless grin, accompanied by his gentle tone, snapped her last threads of control and she wept outright.

He gave her a box of tissues and sat down. "Your other teeth are actually in quite good shape," he said, offering consolation.

Undesired. Discarded. A mouth full of rotting teeth.

Her weeping did not abate and Dr. Adin grew uneasy. His next two patients were waiting in the front room, rattling their magazines nervously and shifting positions in their chairs as the sound of sobbing reached them.

"Margaret, it's going to be all right." He patted her shoulder. "We'll fix your teeth. You can pay in instalments, something you can manage until you're back on your feet."

Meekly, gratefully—spent—she nodded. She blew her nose, pushed her hair out of her face and stood up. She hadn't realized she'd been clenching her muscles during the whole appointment. She was stiff and her clothes were damp from perspiration.

"Make an appointment with the receptionist. Remember, twice a day," he said, holding up the dental floss as though to remind her of her part of the bargain.

TWO

The irritating drone of a neighbour's lawn mower penetrated Margaret's sleep on Saturday morning and brought in its wake a brief memory of the dentist's drill. She slid back into her dream.

She's in a country cottage. There's been a big storm and all the lines are down. It's getting dark outside. She wants to turn a light on, but no matter how gently she turns the switch, it won't catch and the light doesn't go on. She tries other lights and none of them work either. She is scared at the thought of being alone all night without lights. She picks up the phone to see if the telephone lines are down too. A male voice speaks her name as though across a great distance. He says he won't be able to fix the lines until tomorrow and she thinks, *I don't want him to know I'm here alone in the house,* so she says, "We're fine," hoping he'll believe a man is with her.

The voice wants to know if she can pay.

An angry, frustrated sound—lawn mowers. She'd perspired while sleeping, in places where skin touched skin—the inside of her legs, her armpits—and the side of her head that lay on the pillow. It was going to be an unseasonally warm spring day.

Now that her husband was gone who could confirm for her every day that the world was real? Who was there to witness her in her cotton nightie twisted round clammy knees, who to smell the morning air blowing in from the sea? Why stop dreaming?

She sank back to sleep.

She woke again in the afternoon. The lawn mower was silent now and she rolled onto her back. Another interminable day in an interminable series, nothing melting into nothing, silence into silence. She tried to fall back to sleep but the comfort of unconsciousness evaded her and she supposed the sleeping pills had worn off.

When she'd got back from the dentist on Monday she'd switched on her answering machine and turned the volume down to zero. She'd taken sleeping pills in the intervening nights and often during the day, too, waking only to eat, go to the bathroom or watch sitcoms and talk shows in the evening. The past eight days, Margaret thought while examining the light fixture on the ceiling, had been like a Surrealist film where the hero's profile is shown in shadow—eye open, eye closed, eye open, eye closed; waking, sleeping, waking, sleeping, day and night passing in an eye blink, occasionally a tear escaping the closed eyelid, the closed shutter.

She rolled back onto her side. A perfect blue sky hung

outside the bedroom window. Without warning tears began streaming down her cheek and round her nose. A wordless moan rose from her chest, naked and raw, so animal that even in her pain she was shy hearing it.

When the weeping passed she lay as before, staring out the window. She couldn't understand why, if they no longer loved each other, the prospect of divorce should hurt so much.

THREE

*I*t hurts so deeply because he never loved you.

She opened her eyes. Spring clouds like amorphous white balloons bobbed across the blue sky. Sunday morning. She closed her eyes.

Looking back now she saw that it had started the first time he'd insisted the lights be turned off. They'd had sex mutely in darkness and afterwards he'd been unusually affectionate and solicitous. Then he stopped touching her breasts, except occasionally as a kind of courtesy, and finally he stopped touching her at all. He bought her a long-sleeved, high-collared nightgown and asked her to wear it when they had intercourse. He fabricated a sexual fetish—"You look like a nun," he said. At other times it was a ghost. The ghost of desire.

She rolled onto her back and opened her eyes again. Dead insects had accumulated in the ceiling light fixture.

She could see their threadlike feelers and legs through the frosted glass. The last three years he'd had sex with her once a month, out of duty, with soft desireless caresses, penetrating her reluctantly, holding himself up on his fists, his face turned away.

"It's not you," he offered as consolation one night. It was his medical practice. Being confronted with the human body, day in and day out. When he looked at people, shook their hands, said "Hello, how are you," he was overwhelmed by repulsive physiological impressions: rattling mucus in the chest, the clammy pungent smell of genitals, ear wax, ragged skin near the cuticles, pimples on the buttocks, dark hair follicles on the backs of arms rising to goosebumps, the odour of warm urine, vomit, sweat, faeces, rot. When he looked at people, their whole biological history rose before his eyes, from the bloody mess of their birth to the morbid sweet smell of their infirmity. He had to strain now to hear what people were saying over the roar of their bodies. Other people, friends from medical school, his mother and his sister, had been irritated by his air of preoccupation, his inattention to their conversation. Margaret tried to understand and be sympathetic.

She'd brought up the subject of children a year or two after they were married; he'd wanted to pay off his student loans first and get established in his practice. She asked about children again a few years later and he was frank. "I can't risk being repulsed by my own child. I couldn't bear that. The smell of that genetically new skin, milky vomit, yellow diarrhoea. I would be unable to show affection. I couldn't do that to a child."

But you can to me. She felt like the shell of a woman.

Bodiless. A mute pair of eyes watching from an internal desert.

She put a foot over the side of the bed and lowered it onto the cool wooden floor. Then the other foot. She stood up. Her joints felt as though they were held together by thread, her bones suspended in the air like a floating mobile. She clicked and creaked over to her chest of drawers like a fragile, somnambulistic exoskeleton.

The mirror revealed oily hair full of rats' nests, kinked at weird angles. She hadn't changed her clothes since Monday and they smelled strongly of skin oils and stale perspiration. She took them off and put on a clean oversized T-shirt and went down to the kitchen. She opened the fridge door and looked inside. Sour milk, coffee cream, all the usual condiments—mustard, relish, jam, etc.—and a pastry box containing a lemon meringue pie. She never ate food like that, old-fashioned bakery food. She'd bought it for comfort and consolation. She cut a big piece, mentally listing all the ingredients that were nourishing—citrus, carbohydrates, eggs, vitamin C, cornstarch. It tasted like cardboard and refrigerator ozone. She made coffee. The first sip warmed her mouth, then her throat.

She carried her coffee into the studio. She hadn't looked inside this room since Friday night when John had come to take his possessions. He'd found a townhouse to rent. Her studio had lost a lamp, a small Persian carpet, a large cactus, and there were gaps in the bookcase that the remaining books had collapsed into.

One of the things she'd been avoiding by sleeping the past eight days away was working on the hummingbird. Even before John left, she'd avoided it. It repelled her in some way. But she was out of bed now and wide awake and she could not afford to procrastinate any longer. She'd checked the calendar, "Monday, April 4—Del. hummingbird." The thing was due tomorrow. She should have phoned the guy at the aviary and told him it was going to be late. She wanted to phone and tell him that she was very sorry but she couldn't do it at all. That she thought it was a very bad idea in the first place to build a giant hummingbird, that the request was oxymoronic since the essence of a hummingbird was to be small and fast and blurred and the idea of creating a giant one negated the very qualities that gave it hummingbirdness. It was just not possible to build a giant hummingbird that would "appear lifelike."

But she needed the money more than ever and so she hoped that, because it was only intended to be suspended from the ceiling of the new souvenir shop and would not be part of any scientific display within the aviary proper, its surreal qualities might be considered quirky, intriguing, some kind of artistic statement.

Appear lifelike.

Removed from life by one. Not-life appearing to be life. She thought of science fiction movies—ectoplasm, alien incubations, demonic succubi, silicone ooze transforming itself into credible representations of human life on earth. Not-life appearing to be life. The back of her throat began to ache as it always did when she was about to cry.

Her life.

The aliens in those films were metaphors for how people really felt about themselves. Strange souls inhabiting body shells.

A tiny stuffed hummingbird sat brilliantly on the worktable. She'd found it after a fruitless search through all the taxidermy shops listed in the Yellow Pages. It had been in a pawn shop, recognizable as a hummingbird only after she'd blown off a thick coat of dust.

She liked the beautiful stuffed thing and thought of it as the "real" hummingbird, though it wasn't really real either. It was a shell too, the shell of a real hummingbird whose hummingbird soul had hovered briefly over its still-warm body, then departed. A taxidermist had carefully sliced open its skin and removed all the flesh inside, transforming it into an emerald feather coat for a tiny fairy king. The taxidermist had then sewn it back up, filled the coat with stuffing, implanted tiny glass eyes, glued its tiny feet to the lacquered stand and set luminescent wings up in the air, poised as though it were caught in slow motion. Time-held. Pinned forever to the present.

Beside the mounted bird on the worktable was the huge blank presence of the giant hummingbird. It looked, with its smooth white skin of plaster, like a giant eggshell with the foetal head, wings, tail and legs growing on the outside. The eyeballs were covered with saran wrap and masking tape. Wire hoops jutted out where the wings would be. It looked so heavy and white. Its whiteness seemed to connote pure fear and absolute burning hatred for everything that caused that fear. It was stranded, wingless and blind, on the wire frame she'd built to keep it upright while she worked, and its white paralysed bulk, its malevolent fear, dominated the room.

She hovered at the doorway, hesitating to enter. The hummingbirds—small and giant—watched her nervously from glassy eyes at the sides of their heads, ready to take off should she move. There was still so much work to be done. Sanding, all the painting, the wings needed to be finished, its beak wasn't set right. Each of these tasks required thousands of tiny decisions and the thought of even one such decision exhausted her. She couldn't even lift her foot past the threshold into the room. She felt like a statue, with no live nerves to transmit messages from her brain to her muscles and instruct them to move. The lines were down. The present moment fell continuously away before her and devoured her puny impulses before a decision to act even formed.

The giant hummingbird stared out at the world through the saran wrap; its will to see was frantic and unflinching, its anxiety intense. It was desperate to know if enemies approached, if it was hunted. By not finishing the wings she'd left it disabled. It foundered on the table, struggling helplessly, trying to see her clearly, see what sadistic creator had reduced its flickering emerald beauty to this white, gravity-stricken, inanimate silence.

She wanted to get the thing over and done with and out of her house, but since she couldn't even bring herself to go into the room she decided to escape to the museum. She often went to the museum on Sunday, sometimes first to the art gallery and afterwards she treated herself to a steak sandwich and a glass of wine at a nearby bistro. She liked being in an anonymous crowd, participating in a shared culture with strangers, eavesdropping on their comments, observing faces and body language. Even so, she often felt a little pained being publicly alone—unclaimed. But the overall feeling of freedom, of being able to live in her own thoughts and act purely on her own whims, to watch people who were too occupied being with someone else to look consciously around them, compensated for it.

She got dressed and stepped out of the house into the breezy April day feeling a little like a taxidermied animal herself, whose soul, mute and anxious, still inhabited the stuffed dead body.

FOUR

Bones as big as buildings. Large unwieldly joints assembled like a child's Meccano set. A giant sloth reared up, exposing a pelvic girdle wide enough to give birth to a sumo wrestler, a rib cage big enough to house a child; it pawed lethargically at the air. If it could, it would bring down clouds, like deer shot in mid-air. Enforce the law of gravity. Bring the sky to the ground.

The dark-brown tibia of some lumbering dinosaur whose pinhead bobbed at the end of a neck long and muscular as a python. What huge plants travelled down that esophagus to fuel its thundering motion? The tibia was six feet tall and shaded brown and black like a very tarnished penny (if time had a colour...), its concave curves and convex knobs the sensual structure of a history of wordlessness and slow turbulence, where Homo sapiens was still too random a possibility to be a twinkle in anyone's eye. The dinosaur bones were like a beautiful hallucinogenic mystery, a creation worthy of an omnipotent God.

The small dark rooms of the museum rumbled with the silence of the extinct bones.

Margaret heard a whimper and turned to see a young boy clutching his mother's leg. The mother tried to pry him loose—"They're just bones Tommy, they can't hurt you. They aren't alive."

Across the room tyrannosaurus rex loomed, jaw gaping open, tiny thalidomide arm stubs sticking out from its chest. The child whimpered louder and begged his mother to take him away. He didn't believe it was dead, couldn't believe in the inanimateness of such huge bones; and the thought of it being alive, running after him, standing over him with that cupboard-sized jaw caused his small heart to despair. He would not be comforted and his mother finally gave up and carried him out.

Margaret progressed through the halls, moving from the prehistoric toward the present, and noticed that the skeletons became smaller and more delicate, as though a creator had reversed the usual process for sculpting and had built giant crude maquettes as practice for later, smaller originals. The gargantuan rib cages, thundering legs, huge stone-toothed jaws were becoming less evident and in their place came a profusion of delicate skeletons: crouching, cowering, grazing, poised to flee. The more recent bones were lighter and had a frail, desiccated look, like the exoskeletons of dead insects.

They reminded Margaret of Giacometti's statues—tiny purposeful figures telegraphing small personal intentions in a huge silent space. Subjectively alone, they were connected to one another through spatial relationship only. They had a whimsical fragility, implausible as physiques meant to survive in the real world.

Margaret entered a marine room where murals of ancient sea life decorated all the walls and the lighting was dim and blue. The huge skeleton of a prehistoric whale was suspended from the ceiling, its vertebrae curved like a sickle, as though it were diving down, jaw open, sharp carnivorous teeth to the front of the mouth and, at the back, teeth that were serrated very oddly and looked like miniature art deco buildings. Floating behind and below the rib cage, unconnected to any other bone, was a vestigial pelvic bone.

The plaque explained that whales, and all other sea mammals, had been land animals who returned to the sea—possibly, in the whale's case, because their skeletons could no longer efficiently support their tremendous weight. The bone structure of the whale's flippers still showed a flattened-out elbow joint and five trailing, elongated fingers.

The words *returned to the sea* filled Margaret with an unexpected nostalgia.

She sat down on a banquette and wondered—had there been a wistful look back, memories of the sound of birds, the feeling of the sun on skin, the pressure of gravity, the touch of a breeze, feet on solid ground? A pull toward the land?

Once exiled, there can never be a complete return home. Something is always being left behind, a slight memory, and there is always a yearning, however repressed, for the life in exile.

People drifted by Margaret's banquette. Adults murmured to one another; children exclaimed insistently to their parents, usually more to get attention than out of true wonder at what they saw. The burble and chirp of video displays echoed intermittently through the halls.

She remembered another afternoon in the museum, gazing at the Neanderthal burial scene. She'd felt someone watching her and when she looked up she almost laughed out loud because he was so startlingly handsome. He didn't smile, but continued to stare at her. He seemed shorter than he actually was because his torso was long and his head large. He made her think of an amaryllis, its huge exotic bloom supported by a leafless stalk, excessive in its most sensual parts.

She remembered seeing Phillip naked. He looked lean and strong, like someone who practised yoga. He had almost no body hair. She remembered his chest, ribs showing through bands of muscle, waiting to press down and touch her. Her hands on his stomach, the muscles of his abdomen taut. She remembered his hot skin in the cool room.

His eyes were an intense burning blue, yet his gaze also had a kind of coolness, a friendly detachment. He seemed interested, gently appraising, inviting a reciprocal appraisal. There'd been an ironic self-consciousness in the way he'd walked toward her across the room.

Why remember Phillip now? Almost a year had passed since their encounter. Only one night, no last names, no addresses. She'd made it clear that their intimacy would be bounded by the beginning and end of that evening. She would not see him again after she got dressed and left.

She hadn't understood yet that her marriage was ending, and she was very clear that she didn't want an affair. But on some level she must have given herself permission to take one night and see what it was like to be desired again, to remember herself before John. She'd returned to her marriage and more or less erased the night from memory.

But there can never be a complete return.

In the next hall a little girl sat exceptionally still in front of a video monitor. An animated mudfish told her how life first moved from the sea onto land. Margaret watched the girl. She looked eleven or twelve years old. Her hands were tucked under her thighs, elbows out, toes pointed in. She was banging her heels against the wooden bench and her mouth hung slightly open.

Margaret remembered the video from her last visit to the museum—the sappy characterization of the mudfish recounting his own story as though it were the plot of a Walt Disney movie. Yet the video had made her think. It made her remember swimming in the warm lakes of Ontario, how wonderful and free she used to feel in the velvet water.

She would forget about her parents sitting on the dock and dive under the surface and swim out as far as she could without coming up for air. All her flying dreams were of swimming through air. Immersed in the lake, all frustration and loneliness fell away; she was pulled by no other desires. In those perfect moments she had everything she wanted; she could float forever.

As she watched the young girl's absorption Margaret wondered what she made of the story. Was she thinking that she was descended from a fish? Was she wondering what physical mutations had occurred to make that happen? The video ended. The girl stared at the empty screen for a moment then got up and walked over to a display of freshwater fossils.

A group of nine or ten people edged into the underwater hall. They had deep suntans and some wore T-shirts with various references to Texas. From the middle of the group Margaret recognized Frank Rice's voice. He was the museum's Chief of Exhibits and he often escaped his office to roam the museum, eavesdropping or giving impromptu tours like this one.

"The architecture of this wonderful museum is simple—a central rotunda from which the halls radiate like the spokes of a wheel, offices and research laboratories on the outer rim." He was tall, with the graceful awkwardness of an amateur basketball player, slightly dishevelled, rosy-cheeked, buoyant.

"As you meander through these halls, it may seem to you that each display follows logically on the one before and that each one is complete and scientifically accurate. Museums create an aura of permanency and stability and even authority. The truth is, here at the National Museum, we're continually improvising. Tinkering, revising, fiddling, updating. I liken the process to evolution itself where every species, no matter how old and stable, is becoming something else, has been something else. The museum is no different than the life you see around you. Transient. Change made concrete.

"We humans," he added, as though it were an afterthought, "are prone to think of ourselves as the final product of evolution. We think of the species preceding us as part of a teleological progression whose sole purpose is to evolve into Homo sapiens. Because we think of ourselves as the goal of evolutionary change, it's easy for us to think the world around us is permanent and stable and forget that we too, however slowly, are either evolving into another species or heading for extinction."

The group was getting restless. One heavy woman nudged her husband and they sidled away to look at an ancient sea turtle. Frank recognized Margaret, waved and signalled for her to wait.

"Well *I'm* just getting warmed up, but you people are here to see the whole museum. I'll leave you to explore. If you have any comments or suggestions please drop me a line." He handed out business cards, then strode over to her.

Normally Margaret would have been pleased to see him, but today she didn't feel up to making casual conversation. She smiled.

"Good luck to bump into you. I was going to phone you anyway. Do you have a couple of minutes?"

Frank led her past a security guard down a long corridor. On one side dark-green filing cabinets lined the wall, on the other doorways opened into tiny offices where desks and shelves were piled high with a miscellany of birds' eggs, stones, animal skins, books, microscopes, gurgling fish tanks, mouse cages, bones, casts and moulds. Someone had a radio tuned to a rock station playing what sounded like The Clash.

"Did you ever meet Neill Hansen when you worked on that last project for us?"

She nodded. She remembered him quite well because she hadn't really liked him. He was obsessed with the details of his work and his obsession seemed to go hand in hand with undisguised disdain for everyone else not similarly obsessed.

"He did the Neanderthal bust in the Physical Anthropology Hall." They side-stepped a stack of boxes with Latin names scrawled on the sides. "And now he's working on a new series of hominid reconstructions for us."

They turned left down a short wide corridor that led to a huge hall. The wall between the corridor and the hall had been completely knocked down. The sound of drills and objects being crashed about gregariously made it difficult to hear.

"This is the back of the old Marine Hall!" Frank shouted.

The toxic smell of burning plexiglass made Margaret try to breathe as shallowly as she could. The hall was illuminated by dark-blue light intended to create a deep underwater effect. A torch aimed at the rivets on an old bathysphere caused an arc of bright orange sparks to rain down. Someone called for a hammer.

Margaret felt drawn to the room, to the energy of the men working together. Their reality seemed more secure than her own, less arbitrary, less tenuous. Frank touched her elbow, indicating they should turn to the right and continue along another corridor.

The next hall was empty. Wires, sockets, plumbing lay bare; new drywall was stacked in the middle of the floor. Frank unhooked a chain across the entrance and ushered her in.

"What you see," he lifted his arms and circled the empty space like Zorba the Greek, "is the new Hall of Human Origins. I've been lobbying our board and the government since I started this job five years ago. What we've got now is pathetic. See that line?" He gestured at a wide rough band halfway up the wall with wires and pipes sticking out. "There'll be two floors. The top floor will be home for the hominids and the bottom will be used for Native American Culture, which is also desperately in need of more space.

"The museum has caseloads of good fossil casts, from Johanson's First Family to Raymond Dart's Taung skull, and I'm having glass display cases built for them. We'll move the Neanderthal burial scene here, such as it is, and Neill's bust. Work's already started on a three-dimensional computer-animated short depicting a day in the life of Australopithecus afarensis, Homo habilis and Homo erectus, and we're building a small theatre to screen it in. But at the rate Neill works it's going to take him years to complete the hominid reconstructions, and I need a new display for the opening next fall. It's got to be ready on time because I've had to fight hard and I don't want to give the board any excuse to cut this project back.

"You've worked on a couple of projects for us now. The miniature dinosaur environment you did was excellent. You work fast and you have the background in human anatomy with your sculpture. What I'm about to propose, however, will be fairly challenging. Scientifically speaking the territory is uncharted—you'd have to do more of your own research and more scientific guesswork. You'd have Neill as a resource person and supervisor—he has an unparalleled knowledge of comparative primate anatomy and a solid understanding of paleoanthropology."

Frank stopped talking and appeared to be waiting for some kind of answer.

"What is the proposal exactly?" Margaret asked eventually.

"Of course. The display I want completed by the fall requires full body reconstructions of a male and female Australopithecus afarensis. That's the same species as Lucy." He looked to see if this reference meant anything to her.

"The fossil named after 'Lucy in the Sky with Diamonds,' right? Yes. I remember learning about it in an anthropology course. It was found in Ethiopia. Donald Johanson. The remarkable thing about it was not only that the skeleton was quite complete for something so old, but also that it had already evolved structurally for walking erect, but its brain was still not much bigger than a chimpanzee's."

"That's right. Our display will centre on the Laetoli footprints. You've heard of them?"

"Mmmm. Vaguely. No, not really."

"The Laetoli footprints are amazing. They're one of the most magical finds in paleoanthropology. They were discovered one day when some scientists from one of Mary Leakey's digs had an elephant dung fight. Three and a half million years old, there they were under soil and sediment. Footprints of three human ancestors walking erect across a bed of ash spewed out by a volcano. It rained and the rain turned the ash into a natural kind of cement. The footprints are even older than the Lucy skeleton, but they almost certainly belong to the same species. They're absolute proof that Australopithecus afarensis walked erect, at least some of the time.

"Neill has already started on the reconstruction of the adult male. I'm hoping you have the next five or six months free to do a reconstruction of the adult female. He'll familiarize you with the necessary primate anatomy and your work will be based on Johanson's Lucy skeleton. There is a large difference in size between the male and female but structurally they are very similar, so you should be able to use a lot of Neill's research."

"Are there any reconstructions of Lucy in other museums?"

"I think there are a few. One in London I believe, New Mexico, New York—but none have been done with the level of research and attention to science that Neill is bringing to his work. I don't think they'll be hard to improve on."

Frank walked over and picked up a chocolate bar wrapper someone had tossed into the hall. He scrunched it up and held it in his hand.

"The great thing is next week the museum is hosting a symposium jointly with the universities on modes of locomotion for Australopithecus afarensis, and one of the speakers is bringing some original fossils of a female. They'll be stored in our labs for a few days. The chance to see one of these fossils firsthand without having to travel to Africa is rare, because of course now they all return to their country of origin."

Original bones. Margaret imagined them in the dry powdery earth of an excavation, slowly unburied, lifted gingerly out. "Who are you?" the paleoanthropologist in khaki shorts and shirt asks the bones, hair unbrushed, face hot and dusty, hand spectacularly aware of contact, the hard dusty feel of an ancestor. "Who am I?" The bones answer question with question.

"So are you interested?" Frank asked.

"Yes," she said and added, smiling, "I'd get to keep my teeth after all."

He raised his eyebrows but did not ask. "Good. There's a meeting of the Hall of Human Origins Committee at nine Friday morning. Can you come?" She nodded. "The budget is as usual restricted but we could offer you the equivalent or perhaps a bit more than last time. I might be able to squeeze some kind of advance if that's helpful." He looked at her intently.

"How *are* you?" he asked. She looked evasively out the door. "You've been unusually quiet."

Margaret hesitated. He would be the first person she'd told.

"My husband and I are splitting up. But really I'm fine. It just takes a little adjusting," she said lightly, trying to smile reassurance.

He gave her shoulder a little squeeze, hesitated, wondering perhaps if he should say more, but decided to accept her reassurance.

"Well all right. See you Friday morning. Take care of yourself."

They had walked across the empty hall to an entrance that led back into the museum's public space. Frank lifted the chain, invited her to duck under, then scissor-jumped over himself, coins and keys jangling. He strode off through the crowds with his loose-limbed gait, tossing the candy wrapper into the wastebasket from an imaginary free-throw line. He turned and waved to her.

Margaret didn't know what to do now. She didn't really feel like wandering through the museum any more, but she didn't feel like going back to an empty house either. She decided to look for the reconstruction of the Neanderthal Neill had done. She didn't remember seeing it on other visits to the museum.

Why hadn't she married someone like Frank? Cheerful, curious, generous, *fun*. No—wrong landscape. She would never fit into Frank's world. She and John were both serious, heavy, like characters in German movies, both not *fun*, both hungry.

The bust was in a small alcove where Native American History ended and Anthropology began and it drew her eye immediately. It was of a completely different order from the reconstructions for the Neanderthal burial scene, which seemed crude and toylike in comparison. Neill had left the grey clay unpainted and had not added hair, yet it seemed more real than the painted, hairy specimens.

Something about its massiveness made Margaret want to touch it. It was sensual, its lips suggested a kiss to her, a caress, and its contours aroused a kind of hedonistic pleasure in her that was oddly intensified by its facial expression. The Neanderthal seemed surprised and pained, as though he'd just realized he was the last one of his species.

FIVE

M argaret suddenly grasped the side of the bed. She felt as though she were falling, as though all the nerves in her body were blocking out the tactile information that there was a bed underneath her. She was plummeting down a black hole. *Where am I?* 1:12 a.m. No John. She drifted back down to sleep.

Small dinosaurs cavort in the dust at her feet.

They crane their long necks. Their heads are cool and smooth and round as a dog's nose and they brush against the bare skin of her ankles. A tyrannosaurus rex runs on miniaturely powerful legs. It ignores a tasty apatasaurus on its right and aggressively charges her ankle, leaping into the air with open jaw. Its mouth is open so wide it can't see where it's going, even though it's already airborne toward her flesh…

A garden, lush and green and damp with mist. She is

sitting on a moss-covered stone beside a magnolia tree. A snake is coiled around the trunk, emerald-green and brown. He offers her the nozzle of a hookah. She takes the pipe in her mouth and sucks smoke in and only then realizes there is no way to exhale. Her body fills with smoke like a balloon, growing bigger and bigger, and she floats up above the trees.

She is growing quite anxious because if she lets her breath out now she'll whoosh down to the ground so fast she'll be dashed to pieces. The smoky air explodes out of her and *whoosh*...

A single-celled being. Tiny creatures with waving cilia swim by. An amoeba projects a foot and traps one of the tiny creatures. It secretes a substance that breaks down the creature's outer membrane. Then the amoeba absorbs it. With great effort Margaret manages to grow a little bigger. The ground shakes. A June bug looms over her then veers suddenly to the right. It attacks a worm and the worm struggles to keep the June bug from killing it.

Her body expands and shrinks as though it exists in a manic zoom lens. She can't hold a stable size even for a second and helplessly fluctuates from microcosmic to gigantic.

SIX

S he woke.

The hummingbird was due.

She went back to sleep.

In the afternoon she got up because someone was phoning her repeatedly. The answering-machine was on and the volume was turned right down because she didn't want to hear the caller's voice, or John's, intoning their message. Still, the phone rang a couple of times before the machine intercepted and those rings were making her anxious. She unplugged the phone, then she went back to bed.

One thing she'd miss about marriage was the feeling of public accompaniment. Of being beside someone. She'd enjoyed having John's parents over for Sunday dinner for example, not because their company was particularly agreeable, but because she liked the feeling of being hosts together, of working side by side. She loved the moment in a movie theatre when the lights had just gone down and the opening credits were rolling and John was beside her, facing the screen. She'd glance at his profile in the reflected light. In the early days she would swing her leg over his and hook her foot under his other knee.

She remembered sometimes being overcome with sudden happiness when the two of them walked down the sidewalk together. She'd fall behind him, then take a couple of running steps and jump up on his back, wrap her arms round his neck and kiss his cheek. The first couple of times he chuckled indulgently and carried her past a few houses before stopping to let her down. Then he'd just stand there patiently waiting for her to slide down again. Then he started complaining, "My neck! It's straining my neck, Margaret. You don't know what stress it causes having an adult woman hurtle up behind you and hang herself on your neck when you're not prepared." And she had let go obediently, believing it was his neck. The last couple of times he just snapped, "Christ don't do that! I thought I explained it to you. My neck can't take it." She'd felt shame but she didn't want to apologize. She no longer believed it was his neck.

Now she questioned why she'd kept jumping up on him after he'd made it clear he didn't like it. Had she been so wrapped up in her own passing joy that she didn't care if his neck hurt or not? She did think the pleasure of receiving her affection should have transcended any discomfort she might inadvertently have caused. What was a little neck pain compared to the upwelling of true love?

The thought that John might never have loved her had hurt, but she was beginning to suspect something even more difficult. She was beginning to suspect she might not have loved him. She'd loved him in the sense of indulging an intense affection, of wanting to be near him, of wanting him, but she doubted she'd ever considered him separate from her own needs. And when his needs didn't coincide with hers she'd resented them, felt wounded by them, abandoned.

If she hadn't loved John, had she ever loved anyone?

That night she watched TV until two in the morning, took a couple of sleeping pills and slept again.

The next morning—Tuesday—she woke early. Ten mornings without John and now she was no longer surprised by his absence beside her in bed, no longer searched confusedly for an explanation.

She dressed quickly and went down to the kitchen. The sound of her sandals clacking on the wooden stairs echoed through the house. She never remembered hearing her own movements in the house so distinctly before, though of course she'd often been there alone. There was silence when she stopped to turn the thermostat up, then her sandals made a softer clatter on kitchen linoleum. The hummingbird. She needed the money for the dentist. And for the mortgage. She just wanted to get the damn thing out. It was such an unpleasant creature.

She poured cereal into a bowl. She poured milk on it. The flakes seemed too dry, despite the milk, too papery and brown. She tried to scupper a couple with spoonfuls of milk. Already she could feel her will to work on the hummingbird fading. She looked out the window at her garden. Random clusters of crocuses were spent, the shrouds of their blooms glued filmily to their leaves. Among the compacted drifts of decaying wet leaves yellowy-green sprouts had broken through. The ground seemed to rumble softly with subterranean growth. Margaret imagined worms industriously depositing brown coils of earth at the mouths of their holes, clearing out their tunnels for spring, preparing for the onslaught of pale roots poking through in a lightless search for nitrogen and other nutrients. Tiny pigmentless slugs tumbled out of slug egg or womb, anticipating marigolds and lettuce.

Her flowerbeds were usually well tended but last year she'd neglected them. Chickweed appeared in sporadic light-green clumps. Yellow dandelions drew sunlight down on their heads. Runners of grass laid claim to unoccupied earth.

She went outside. The sun was warmer than she'd expected for April. Its heat penetrated her clothes. She was struck by the freshness of hearing sounds not generated by herself—birds singing, the diffuse rushing sound of free air, car tires on asphalt, a lawn mower running over a stick. She felt reassured by them, relieved that the world existed outside of herself.

On the stairs of the back porch was a columbine she'd bought just before John left. It had enchanted her, an old-fashioned flower from the time when ladies wrote long letters to one another and were friends for life.

She saw that one of the blooms was open, and she crouched down to look more closely. It was colourful and exotic and reminded her somehow of a nun. Perhaps because of its wings, the flaps and tendrils all sticking out crisply at angles. The flower's sex was in the centre, a bouquet of yellow seeds on sticky stamens cloaked by a hood of yellow petals which were capped by deep-red wings, the airborne part, the red fairy's hat. A tiny brown bug was taking liberties among the seeds, wandering from one delicate cluster to another. Sensing her presence it scooted out of sight into the hidden roots of the stamens.

The plant had survived several weeks being watered only by rain, but it hadn't rained in a week and the earth in the small pot was dry and had shrunk from the edge. She put on her gardening shoes and an old gardening hat and carried the columbine to a spot between two clumps of irises. She knelt in the small world of shadow the hat created round her. Above, last year's rosehips knocked dryly in the breeze. Delicate burgundy leaves sprouted from green branches. Last summer its huge red roses could only be seen from the second floor because neither she nor John had pruned. They'd both stopped doing much around the house. The lawn got mowed but not weeded or aerated. Shingles weren't repaired, eavestroughs weren't cleaned. The rosebush now stood over ten feet high and had become a chaotic tangle of the quick and the dead.

She dug several trowelfuls of dirt and piled it to the side, picking out larger stones and bits of crockery. Every spring it seemed a new assortment of broken china and stones surfaced on her flowerbeds. She remembered how she'd first learned why this was so, but she didn't remember where she'd come across the story, or if it was apocryphal.

Two lovers in the Soviet Union, desperate for privacy, went out into the country. They found a field lying fallow, and as they wandered looking for a spot to spread their blanket they stumbled across a huge marble head breaking through the soil among the grass and wildflowers. They made love by its right cheekbone, excited by the voyeurism of its stone gaze, then informed officials at the city hall of the nearest town that a statue was rising out of the field.

It was Stalin. Twenty years earlier villagers had carted it out to the field, dug a huge hole and buried it, forever, they thought. But now it had floated back up to the surface. They were uneasy about its reappearance until they learned that stone was lighter than earth.

The hole for the columbine was almost deep enough when she noticed something writhing at the bottom. It was a half-worm, its severed body frantically searching for the rest of itself. Even as she recoiled and wondered nervously where the other half was, hoping it was not anywhere near her, she felt anguish for the worm and thought there must be pain. The sight of the pinky brown end waving in the air, not knowing in which direction to travel, was unbearable. She lifted it onto the trowel and tossed it behind the irises. If birds didn't find it first, the worm could regrow its lost half. She tossed some more earth over it and tried to forget it was there.

There was no escape from pain. Even here, in the peace and beauty of the garden.

Half a self lying every morning divorced on the mattress: an arm, a leg, an eye, an ear—a divorced Noah's ark sailing to the end of life with only one of everything, its past and future amputated. Her house half-filled with furniture, half the necessary kitchen utensils, half the pictures gone, half of everything missing. Divorce was very physical. She felt so vulnerable now even walking down the sidewalk, or talking to friends. She was at the stage before the missing parts started to grow back, the writhing, confused stage. Root, living terror.

She pried the columbine from its pot. A white web of roots held the soil in the shape of the pot. She placed it in the hole and found that the hole needed to be deeper and wider at the bottom, so she lay the columbine on the grass and began scooping more earth out. Something whitish fell in. A tiny bone. It was porous and light, no knobs or joints, slightly curved. A rib.

Gently she scratched the wall of the hole where she thought it had fallen from until she found another whitish object. As she excavated around it with her fore-finger, the roots of the iris tubers tickled her knuckles.

The second bone was a tiny skull with the upper part of a beak attached. Robin-sized, she thought. The skull was filled with dirt—no maggots or flesh that Margaret could see. The fine bone around the eye sockets and at the base of the skull had broken and chipped, but other-wise it was intact. Two pea-sized holes about a quarter-inch apart made her think perhaps it had been killed by a BB gun.

She imagined the bird at night, scaly feet holding a branch deep inside a fir tree, watching shadow and wind play with each other, tucking its head against its breast to sleep. The fragile skull whispered of a terror-stricken moment, a sad ending. She put the skull aside on the grass.

She dug another hole and planted the columbine, sat-urated it with water then pressed earth firmly around its base. She left the first hole open so she could come back later and look for more bones. She wanted to clean the dirt out of the bird's skull and look at it more closely, but also she felt ready, finally, to enter her studio and begin work on the hummingbird.

As she carried the tiny rib and skull back into the house, an image floated through her mind of a skull with a columbine planted inside the cranium. The intricate flowers bloomed through the eye sockets, and its roots grew out through the neck: the past containing the present while the present gradually eroded it and turned its losses into dust.

The air in her studio was dormant and smelled of plaster and clay and glue. She put the bird's skull on the filing cabinet. A few clumps of wet dirt spilled out. The skull seemed so delicate and fragile, so alive in contrast to the hulking, mummified form stranded on her worktable.

She decided not to listen to the messages on her answering-machine but just to phone the director of the aviary and tell him she was still intending to deliver.

"To not even have the courtesy or the professionalism to call and tell me it would be late is unacceptable. I can tell you right now you won't be working for me again. When *will* it be ready?"

"Tomorrow," she answered impulsively. She hadn't really figured out how long the work would take. "Tomorrow afternoon."

"Call me when it's done," he said and hung up.

She didn't know how to begin, how to approach the bird's whiteness, its blank skin. She began to talk herself through each step with short plain instructions.

"Pry open the paint cans... Where's the screwdriver? What colour do you need first?... Find the mixing jars... Clean the airbrush nozzle."

The trick would be to mix a hot green and fleck it with turquoise and gold. Glowing. Average body temperature 105 degrees Fahrenheit.

"Up to 114 degrees," she murmured to herself. "How hot would its body feel in your hand?"

Their tiny chokeberry hearts beat five hundred to twelve hundred times a minute. The wings flutter so fast they look translucent to the human eye.

"Fill the airbrush. You need a mask unless you want green-speckled lungs."

Why do they need to move so quickly? Flowers aren't going anywhere. They have the highest metabolism of all birds. They eat more, relative to their body weight, than any other vertebrate.

Why? They move fast so they can eat a lot. They eat a lot so they can move fast. There is no purpose. They might survive just as well eating less and flying slower.

The reason must be—in order to be hummingbirds. As though evolution's purpose—no, it doesn't have a purpose—evolution's *effect* were to create as much variety as the earth could support. Difference for its own sake. For the sake of beauty.

It was all flesh and blood though, all integument and bone and sinew, all the same clay fired with the same spark.

"Keep your hand slow and steady. Apply evenly." Her arm was tired and she rested.

A metabolism too fast for memory. A hummingbird's present is gone before it can snag onto the past and be remembered. Hummingbird moments vanish as they occur—hot and impenetrable. They burst through time, embodiments of the ephemeral. They live only slightly longer than insects.

She began again, fading the green slowly toward the wings. The rhythm of the work absorbed her. She mixed colours for the belly—buff, soft brown, whites. The afternoon passed timelessly. She sprayed black under the beak and made it blend into the green. She switched to oil paints and brush for the brilliant fuchsia gorget. A bejewelled bird. When she finished the neck she set the brush in turpentine and looked up from her work. It was dark out.

After dinner and with a fresh cup of coffee she returned to the studio. She hesitated at the doorway.

Painted, with the eye unbound, it was amazing how different the bird looked. The white spot behind the eye seemed to accentuate the bird's anger, even malevolence—a glittering vindictiveness. The truth was hummingbirds were very aggressive. Thirty-five percent of their waking hours were spent in belligerent displays, swooping down on each other with long sharp claws eager for each other's flesh, beaks poised to poke at the other's eye. On such a large scale it was impossible to hide its true nature.

She set her coffee down and walked round to the other side of her worktable, where the bird's eye was still bound in plastic and tape. The covered eye made the model look completely different—vulnerable, tragic, as though, like Oedipus, it had been struck down by fate.

The bird's duality reminded her of John. Sarcastic, hostile, disappointed—above all disappointed. It never occurred to him to try to change what was disappointing him—his practice, her, himself; he just sank into resentful hostility.

Then the covered eye—underneath the plastic and tape another side of John facing her. Three years ago she'd called a cab and rushed him to Emergency; he was gasping with pain, sweating, dizzy, he didn't know what was happening. He was rushed into an examining room and the next time she saw him he was lying on a trolley in a green hospital gown with an IV hooked up and a clear plastic tube running out of his nose. He looked right in her eyes. They'd given him some morphine and he was sinking into a calm euphoria, but he still knew he was in danger and helpless. He looked at her with complete trust; she would look out for him. There was no doubt and no measurement of this bond. It was just there.

They'd had a couple of poppyseed squares from a European bakery for dessert. As she watched the poppyseeds zip out his nose and down the tube, she realized he did have her absolute loyalty; she would be vigilant until he was through this. She was surprised because the appendicitis attack happened when their marriage already seemed dead. They weren't talking any more, except to make observations about the newspaper, the weather, their food.

She removed the plastic from the other eye and painted around it. When she thought of John she blamed him for her loneliness, for the pain she was in, for her inability to face much more than getting out of bed each day, for her bewilderment and fear. But blame implied choice, and she wondered, did he have a choice? Could it have been different?

For example, she had chosen to marry John of her

own free will. She had thought she could get what she needed from him. But in retrospect the choice was made blindly; she had no control over and little insight into what impelled it. She didn't know in advance what the outcome might be. Free choice was still subject to contingency; it didn't mean you were in control of your destiny. But if you weren't in control how could you be responsible for the outcome? And if the choice was always mostly blind, how could you blame anyone? How could you say either of them was responsible for the failure of the marriage? Still she felt guilty. And still she blamed John.

Resentful. Malevolent. Helpless. Afraid. One side struggling to see, struggling for insight and control, the other side not caring, angry and looking for revenge.

By midnight she was ready to start the wings. She'd already constructed the individual spines of each feather and attached them to the wing bone. She spread a bolt of purply-taupe silk gauze over her worktable. She would stretch it between the spines of each feather and cut an overlap which she would glue underneath the next feather. Then the whole wing would be painted with satin-finish varathane and the curved tip of each feather shaped from the stiff gauze with scissors. The effect she hoped to achieve would be of gossamer flight, a slightly blurred impression of speed.

She was tired, yet the hours of uninterrupted work had left her feeling peaceful and a little light-headed, almost giddy. She sifted the gauze through her fingers, letting it fall in shimmering folds on the table. She had an impulse to drape the fabric over her shoulders, which she did and, having done that, found herself wrapping it around like a toga. She went to the bathroom to look in the mirror, expecting a glamorous reflection, a goddess. *Mirror, mirror on the wall...*

The material was so light and thin that she looked more like a fly wrapped in a web. She took the end that hung over her shoulder and wrapped it round her face. She looked like a creature from the spirit world, silent, mysterious, boneless, a mummified bride, hovering before the mirror. An androgynous voice began to speak from her, as though the unconscious had come up for air, or an oracle were throwing seeds of the future into the wind.

"*Where you come from, that is where you'll return.*"

"From dust to dust?" she asked her image.

"*No. Only the present is real. Even a bone is only a dream. The dream of a skull, a skull dreaming.*"

"All that is solid melts into air?" she quoted Marx.

"*No,*" replied the cocooned oracle from her veiled and softly bound mouth. "*Who are you? No one. There is only one being. People are variations on a theme.*"

"The collective unconscious?"

"*You are a collection of fragments of that being. You must not worry about being separate; it doesn't matter.*"

"God is one?"

The oracle departed, leaving a silence deeper than the mere absence of sound. The gauze fell from her face and she felt silly swathed in the hummingbird's prospective wings.

SEVEN

"A museum is a gathering place for dead objects." Frank Rice poured ice water into his glass from a jug on the table. "Everything here has been stolen from its real context and placed in a kind of limbo, deprived of its natural right to decay. Preserved. And turned into a static dead object.

"Why do people go to museums? They go to see natural wonders. They're drawn to strange, slightly macabre relics, like mummies. They want to see the secrets of the past. They come to be enlightened. They come for a religious experience. They come to discover some esoteric truth about the world.

"How do we satisfy their desires?" Frank opened his eyes a little wider. The meeting room was small and dingy. The paint on the walls was darkened by grime and age, the finish on the floorboards had long since worn off and the grouting round the windowpanes had chipped and cracked. The meeting table was solid oak while the chairs everyone sat on were a miscellany of plastic kitchen chairs, desk chairs and lab stools.

In attendance were the chairman of the board and eight members of the Human Origins Committee: Frank, Frank's assistant, a staff paleontologist, an exhibit designer, a staff writer, a representative from a 3-D computer animation house, Neill Hansen and Margaret. Neill and the writer seemed bored, as though they'd heard this speech before, while the designer, the 3-D guy and the paleontologist seemed interested, if somewhat confused about where it was leading.

"We create stories around the artifacts. We recreate the natural context of our artifacts and we place them in history, so that when visitors leave they feel as though they've seen and understood the thing itself. We bring dead objects back to life through the imagination, through *story*."

Margaret leaned her head heavily into her palm, her elbow propped against the table. Her eyes had puffy bags beneath them. Her shirt was wrinkled, her socks didn't quite match, her earrings were silver when gold would have done better, and her lipstick was smeared in one corner of her mouth.

I can barely hold my arm straight to support my head, she thought. *I need sleep. I must look like hell.*

You are no one, the oracle's voice still echoed from Tuesday as though some ghost were wandering across her synapses. It was not her own voice yet not exactly someone else's either.

She felt unattractive and rumpled and insecure. Her

grandmother on her father's side, who prided herself on her continental elegance, had said about her grand-daughter, "You're *attractive* dear, not beautiful but attractive," and though Margaret had understood it was meant as a criticism she'd been content with the assessment. She had long wavy light-brown hair and brown almond-shaped eyes that in sunlight were shot with streaks of green and gold. Her mouth was large though not voluptuous—slightly voracious looking. Her lips were quite red. She wasn't glamorous, yet she wasn't rugged either. More like a hard-angled Pre-Raphaelite.

She wondered if she'd be adequate to the task of reconstructing the australopithecine, and she was already sensing aloofness and contempt from Neill. Her insecurity had started yesterday as she'd overseen the transfer of the giant hummingbird into the aviary's truck and she'd known it wasn't very good. It looked too lumpy and egg-shaped to be capable of flight, and it also looked vindictive and nasty. She wasn't surprised when the director phoned to say he couldn't use it, and if he couldn't use it, he couldn't approve the issue of a second cheque. He didn't ask her to fix it or do another one.

"Footprints," Frank grabbed his chairback for emphasis, "in the hardened ash of time. These will be the basis for our story, as most of you already know." Frank took a deep breath. Neill looked out the window with an irritated sigh. "Three of our ancestors walked across the Laetoli plains 3.6 million years ago, just after a volcano had showered them with ash. This ash contained carbonatite making the ash harden to a natural cement when it rained, leaving us this incredible record of their passing."

Dust into dust, echoed the voice. Ash into ash. No one into nothing. She imagined walking naked across a bed of light flaky ash—poof...poof...poof...soft clouds rose and settled. Everything around her was covered in ash—ash trees, ash stones, ash grass.

"The smaller hominid, which we are guessing was female, paused at one point and turned slightly to the left. This moment of hesitation..." Frank hesitated, searching for words, "is so poignant, pregnant, communicating a feeling of doubt or uncertainty in that creature across three and a half million years—it's an incredibly evocative moment."

Only the present is real, the voice intoned like an oboe solo rising out of a symphony orchestra. Only the moment, the hesitation, the empty space between impulse and action. Margaret felt her feet stop for a moment to gaze at the ash world around her, all colour transformed to grey, all texture feathersoft, almost softer and lighter than air.

"It seems that the 'female'," Frank continued, "and one of the two larger individuals which we are presenting as an adult male, might have even been touching each other in some way as they walked, arm in arm, or one with its arm around the other. The footprints are very close beside each other and vary on their path from side to side almost identically. For the purposes of this display, however, we are choosing to place the female, in her 'moment of hesitation,' with the male a step or two ahead on the original path. The third set of footprints that lie under the 'male's' we will refer to only in the storyboard. We will not do a reconstruction for them because they are somewhat indeterminate and frankly, we don't have the budget. Angela has some ideas about the footprints." Frank gave the floor to the exhibit designer.

A footprint is like a dream, the past insinuating itself into the present. A footprint is a trace of being, left behind like Cinderella's glass slipper. Margaret continued walking in the world of ash while the exhibit designer explained her idea for an interactive display where people could "walk in the footsteps of their ancestors."

Neill cleared his throat. "I have a problem with the display. If we have an adult male and an adult female travelling together they will look like a couple, which is almost certainly misleading. No other great ape has a monogamous mating system, and for that matter 80 percent of *human* societies are polygamous. Furthermore, and this is the strongest argument against it, the degree of sexual dimorphism is much too pronounced in afarensis. The male is at least one foot taller than the female and nearly twice the body weight. Monogamous pair-bonding is found only when the male and female are close in size."

Neill spoke with an unpleasant belligerence, as though expecting irritating or silly objections.

"What about a consort situation?" Margaret asked, then instantly regretted speaking. She was not up to any kind of articulation this morning. "Like chimpanzees."

"What's that?" asked the writer.

"The male forces a female who's in estrus to go off alone with him for several days so he can mate exclusively with her. The females are almost always reluctant to go and have to be bullied. They hang back and try to return to the group. Perhaps this model might provide one explanation for the female's 'moment of hesitation.'"

"I doubt most people are capable of distinguishing the subtle differences between a consort relationship and a modern nuclear family," Neill said contemptuously.

Margaret shrugged and retreated back to the ash world she'd been day-dreaming about. She veered left, away from the track of the male. Raindrops plopped silently into the ash and beaded like mercury before dissolving. The grass underneath the ash was straw-yellow and grazed to the bone. The raindrops augured a change of season, a metamorphosis from grey to green, a billion plump shimmering bodies sacrificing themselves to the dust, and out of this—a brief growing season, enough food for a female hominid to survive another year. A bird flew across her path into a tree and caused a small flurry of ash to float to the ground.

Who are you? the voice asked, and Margaret couldn't tell if it was she who was being addressed in the meeting room or the australopithecine in her ash world.

"I agree with you completely, Neill. You make a strong argument and your points can't be ignored," Frank said. "On the other hand, I don't know how to solve the problem unless we scrap the footprints as the founding principle of the display, which I'd be really reluctant to do. If there's a way to clearly establish a consort relationship over a monogamous one, maybe that's a way to go. With the footsteps following almost the exact variations parallel to one another, it will be hard to justify placing the male at a completely separate point in the tracks. Let's look into other ways we might dissociate the male and the female so they don't appear to be travelling together.

"We've got a tight schedule. Neill's almost finished his preliminary research and he and Margaret should be ready to start their reconstructions by next week. The 3-D computer animation will also have to progress quickly to be ready by fall."

After the meeting Neill suggested Margaret accompany him to the lab where he could demonstrate his recent research in the comparative anatomy of chimpanzees, gorillas and humans. Margaret agreed on condition that she could pick up two coffees from the cafeteria on the way.

The lab was a large room in the basement with stainless-steel tables, sinks, lots of counter space and walls of huge storage drawers. Neill opened a vacuum-locked door to a freezer room.

There were shelves along the walls holding various-sized bodies wrapped in plastic. Neill peeked under the plastic of one, then wheeled a steel trolley beside it. At the end of the refrigerated room he took hold of four chains hanging from an H-shaped joint that ran on two ceiling tracks. The crossbar of the "H" moved sideways so the chains could be pulled to either side of the room. Neill pulled the chains to the body beside the trolley, put hooks attached to each chain through an eye at each corner of a canvas sling underneath the body and winched the sling up. He moved it over the trolley, lowered it and detached the hooks, then wheeled the plastic-wrapped body out into the lab.

A row of plaster casts of chimpanzee heads caught Margaret's eye. It was as though dying had been the culmination of some long, excruciating labour. Their faces were scrunched up and folded in on themselves in a perpetual grimace, their brows collapsed over their eye sockets, their snouts pushed forward, teeth clenched, lips parted. They looked as though they'd been holding onto life fiercely and it had been torn from them.

"How did they die?" Margaret asked.

Neill shrugged. "Some were pretty old. About half from disease. I had one that drowned in a moat."

The lab had the sharp, oily smell of formaldehyde, though Neill's corpses were frozen not preserved.

"I only work with frozen cadavers," he said. "Formaldehyde changes the tissues. I can't get as accurate measurements."

The smell reminded Margaret of the first time she'd seen a cadaver. On her second date with John in the medical school lab. He was doing a dissection and she'd asked if she could see the corpse. This was the term before her anatomy course at art school. She remembered the snap of latex as John got his surgical gloves on.

The corpse was a woman in her early fifties. He had already dissected and reassembled her so he merely had to unfold the skin and lift the organs out. He laid them on the woman's chest and told Margaret how they worked. She imagined having her own organs laid on her body, outside, after she was dead.

John inserted a probe in the womb, then through the cervix and out the vagina—to shock her perhaps, but no, she thought, he really just wanted to show her how everything connected. He kept checking with her to make sure she was okay and she kept saying she was fine. She really did feel privileged to have access to the cadaver. Was she shocked?

No. Yes. She wouldn't let herself be. She was determined not to be squeamish.

The woman was slim yet Margaret had been surprised how greasy the body was; there seemed to be deposits of yellow fat everywhere. Neill opened the female chimp and removed her digestive organs to show Margaret the form of the thorax which was more conical in chimpanzees and Lucy than in humans. He explained how the form of the thorax influenced the shape of the muscles of the trunk. The chimpanzee's fat looked whiter and there was much less of it.

"The papers I gave you include photocopies of my dissection notes," Neill said. "You can come anytime and take her out, but obviously put her back together when you're finished. I've taken casts of most of the layers of the dissection. Some are here and the rest are in my studio."

Margaret was still tired and unable to concentrate on what he was saying. She drifted back to her own thoughts. She remembered when John had uncovered the woman's face. Her head was shaved. There were lines where the skin had been cut: one incision started at the bridge of the nose and went over the top of the head to the base of the neck, another circled the whole crown going across the brow, one went from the corners of the mouth to the base of the jaw and another went from the back of one ear along the scalp to the back of the other ear. The woman's expression had not been like the chimpanzees' at all; it was calm—not peaceful so much as neutral.

The dissection of the face shocked her much more than John's probe poking out of the vagina. The deconstruction of the woman's face seemed a violation.

John peeled back the skin of the cheek and named the muscles and tendons of the face. He carefully lifted an eyeball from its socket and pointed out the nerves feeding back to the brain. He lifted the muscles of the lips and chin to show her the roots of the teeth. After all that lifting of layers she felt as though she'd lost something forever. Like the moment in a science fiction movie when the latex mask of what one thought was a human being is peeled off and an intricate computer is revealed inside. She felt duped, fooled by appearances, by skin, by faces, into thinking humans had a unique identity, a self. In some way *she* felt violated.

John folded the woman's face back together and it regained its dispassionate expression, but for Margaret the woman had become an organic machine, her face a flesh mask.

Neill was now describing how the pelvic bone of Australopithecus afarensis was evolutionarily intermediate between a chimpanzee and a human. Margaret tried to listen but she couldn't concentrate. She told Neill about the morning she saw her first cadaver.

"It was a Sunday, and afterwards John had arranged a brunch to introduce me to some of his friends.

"The lab had brains in plastic ice-cream containers, a heart in an old Corningware dish with the little blue flowers, there were legs and arms wrapped in green garbage bags and I thought it was very surreal. I didn't think I was bothered by it until brunch. It was *dim sum*, which I'd never had before, and everything was coated in this white slippery dough and filled with indeterminate bits of animal meat. When we left the restaurant I started burping and the burps had a strong aftertaste of formaldehyde. I couldn't stop. I burped until I went to bed. I guess they were kind of hysterical burps."

She laughed. Neill, irritated at being interrupted, responded with a begrudging "Hmmm."

"It was her face that really bothered me. When you cut up the face and show the mechanics, it's as bad as thinking of the soul as just a bunch of chemical responses in the brain. There's something very empty and depressing about it."

Neill did not encourage Margaret to go on. He wrapped the chimp back up in its plastic and asked her to hold the freezer door open. He wheeled the trolley in, transferred the chimp to its shelf and winched the cadaver of a gorilla onto the trolley.

A woman in a white lab coat leaned in through the door and told Neill his mother was on the phone.

"You can see what I've done if you want," he said after they had wheeled the trolley out. He handed her a scalpel and left. She sat down beside the gorilla and yawned.

Even frozen there was a slight smell from the gorilla's hair. Where had it come from? Since it was frozen it must have been from a zoo or primate centre. Not from the wild. Not killed by poachers. She'd read about poachers killing gorillas just to cut off their heads and hands as trophies to sell to tourists. The hands were made into ashtrays. Gorilla hand, palm up, supplicant, someone stubbing a cigarette out on its palm in a mimicry of torture. It reminded her of images from the Holocaust, lampshades made of human skin, piles of human teeth harvested for gold fillings. She'd heard recently that the lampshades were apocryphal, but it seemed irrelevant because the image expressed so precisely what was being done to Jews and Gypsies, communists, homosexuals and other "enemies" of the Nazis.

She wondered about the gorilla hand ashtrays, if they were apocryphal too, but it didn't matter.

Humans were strange. To want such trophies in one's house. One's own artifacts. Like a shark's jaw, or a fossil. Something powerful brought down. Dead hands. Hands that held death. Hands that touched death. Explored other people's sick bodies. Those hands had touched her body.

Had she dreamed it? John touching her breasts for the first time that afternoon. He'd come up to her room in the rooming house for tea. They'd kissed. Or rather he kissed her. Passionately, while she was still tasting formaldehyde and burping. They were sitting on a sofa. He unbuttoned her shirt, asking first if it was all right. She said yes, but she hadn't really thought about it. He cupped her breasts in his trembling hands. Had they trembled? Something about him trembled. He leaned forward and put his lips over her nipple and looked up at her and it disturbed her to have him looking up at her that way, perhaps because it was so submissive, or so childlike. Despite her recurring burps, it didn't seem to occur to him that she might still be thinking about the corpse, that images of dead body parts in plastic bags and food containers might be juxtaposed in her mind with his foreplay. She felt guilty that at such an intimate moment all she could think about were the stiff yellow mounds that had been peeled away with the skin of the chest when he'd opened the rib cage.

On their next date she confessed what she'd been thinking and he withdrew, calmly, without reproach, and didn't try to touch her for a while. She appreciated his reserve. After a few more dates she'd finally kissed him.

For their honeymoon John's uncle had invited them to stay at a guest cabin on his ranch. They swam in a river whose water was red from the earth, red and opaque so she couldn't see her toes or legs when she was treading water. She remembered John's leg rising to the surface. Wanting him to touch her in the red water. The sensation of skin touching skin underwater, one sensation layered on top of the other, warm on cool, floating in lighter gravity.

They found a spot on the bank, in the mud. She remembered wanting him closer and closer, wanting him inside her skin, under her skin, wanting to cut herself open and wrap her flesh round him, wanting to give herself totally over to him, to lose herself and drown all pain and fear.

They dropped acid that trip. An old high school buddy of John's had slipped it to him at their wedding. She'd never taken it before and John hadn't since high school. They laughed about the gift because it was so out of character for them, but they took it because they felt carefree and adventurous and like doing something different together. She remembered laughing hysterically about some minnows swimming upstream, nicknaming one of them "Rocky" and this being very funny.

Neill returned from his phone call and they began examining his dissection of the gorilla. She glanced down at one of its arms, the one that hadn't been dissected. It lay by the animal's side and looked alive, as though he might wake up soon. The hand was palm up, fingers curled over, thumb lightly turned in, the hugely callused knuckles visible. She felt sad for the gorilla who was gone and for its life, which could not have been sweet in gorilla terms. She felt an urge to place her hand inside his and hold it, kindly, forever.

Her husband's hands. Hands that later forgot themselves and began performing examinations instead. Once he'd actually started taking her pulse without thinking, then dropped her hand. *Does this hurt? Does this hurt? Do you feel any pressure here?* She hadn't answered truthfully then as she'd laughed.

EIGHT

S he had a strange dream.

On the passenger side of a truck's cab sits a skinny truck driver in his fifties with strawberry-blond hair. His boss sits beside him in the driver's seat. The driver's telling the boss, who has grey hair and wears an elegant white dinner jacket, that he and the boss's mistress had sex. He's somewhat sheepish but he doesn't think the boss is going to be really upset because it happened during an errand they were doing for the boss, and they didn't do it out of lust but out of despair, out of a shared sense of submission to the boss, and out of bored compassion.

The boss, however, takes out a gun and shoots him in the head.

Then he telephones his mistress at her hotel room. He tells her, "I'm picking you up in fifteen minutes. Do a good job on your make-up. I want you to look perfect." She has platinum-blond hair and brown eyes.

The mistress is Margaret, yet in the dream she always thinks of her in the third person—"she" never "I."

There are four people in the boss's limousine: the boss, Margaret, another woman who is possibly a prostitute and another man who is a middle-of-the-road rock 'n' roll singer and reminds Margaret of Billy Joel or Phil Collins.

The boss orders her to take off her shirt. Her naked breasts are beautiful and warm and tanned. The boss tells the other man to touch her breasts if he wants, and so he reaches back from the front seat and caresses them.

The experience is very erotic for Margaret. The excitement of a stranger...the forbidden...the beauty and heat of her own body.

The boss tells her to put her shirt back on. He tells her to fix her make-up. It must be perfect. And suddenly she realizes he's going to kill her. In retrospect she realizes that she already knew when he told her to take off her shirt in front of another man. Even earlier, in fact, when he phoned her and there was more menace than usual in his voice and an absence of words, of sex, just the command. He meant to kill her then. She gets her purse from under the front seat, takes out a compact mirror and lipstick and begins applying it to her lips.

She sees her eyes in the little mirror and in them the sudden comprehension of the reality of what she is doing—this moment—carefully moving lipstick over her skin, making the red outline of her mouth faultless so that in a few hours, after she is dead and her lips are cool as clay, they will look beautiful. She is putting lipstick on, conscious that it is for the last time.

She thinks she must find a way to record this moment, it is so unusual and ripe and bizarrely meaningful otherwise no one will ever know it occurred. A disembodied voice in the dream tells her to "remember and record" the dream after it is over. She sneaks her sketchbook and pencil out of her purse and quickly draws her perfectly made-up face with the knowledge of her own imminent murder in her eyes.

The boss pulls up in front of the other man's apartment. The other woman gets out and walks away. She's wearing short shorts, nylons, heels. The other man gets out too. He's aroused from touching Margaret's breasts and considers following the woman but the boss reminds him that she's part of the boss's overall plan. He wants symmetry. Two women must be murdered.

Soon the boss will shoot her in the heart, leaving her face untouched. He wants her to look beautiful after she's dead so people will know he had a beautiful mistress and it meant nothing for him to kill her.

The menace of the dream followed Margaret into wakefulness, yet the menace was also accompanied by a strange exhilaration. She could still feel the hot flush of sexual pleasure at having her naked breasts touched in the car, and she felt a bracing intellectual clarity.

Something from *Hamlet* was floating through her mind. She didn't know exactly what the reference was but it niggled, and because she thought it might be a clue to the dream's meaning she started looking for it in her collected Shakespeare. Eventually she found the passage. Hamlet speaking to the skull of Yorick, the court jester of his childhood. "Now get you to my lady's chamber," he says to the skull, "and tell her, let her paint an inch thick, to this favour she must come; make her laugh at that."

Every layer was cosmetic, a mask, except the skull. Underneath was the essential self—a skeleton.

Death was everywhere, and the only thing one could hold against it was a moment and the record of that moment. The rest was a mask floating in the sky, clouds passing breezily behind empty eye sockets. Absolute isolation. Absolute stillness. Absolute oblivion.

The feeling of intellectual clarity came in part from the moment when she, the mistress, had gazed into her little mirror. There'd been a kind of infinity. Life was made of just such tiny, impermanent moments of consciousness, moments which, though they could be remembered and recorded, ended irrevocably and had firm boundaries like a stone, and could therefore be said to exist forever, complete and free. For people time was not a river, but more like ellipses in a sentence—discrete, finite, discontinuous, though—and this was the painful part—seductively suggestive of open-endedness.

Remember and record, the voice had said. A premonition that an ephemeral experience might be preserved and continue past the life that contained it like an arrow shot past death. Like footprints 3.6 million years ago, footprints of a creature long dead.

NINE

Margaret spent the next three days reading books on Australopithecus afarensis, on the Lucy find, and studying Neill's notes on comparative anatomy and skeletal structure. She was happy not to have to go outside or talk to anyone. She wanted uninterrupted time to think and begin to recreate her sense of her future separate from John and his life. She went to the store once for groceries and a newspaper but otherwise just puttered in the garden and read and made notes. As Margaret thought about the structure of afarensis's body and reread her notes, an image of Lucy was beginning to form in her mind.

Tuesday morning she settled into her armchair to do some more reading. The refrigerator shuddered to a stop and the house was silent. A light rain fell outside. The telephone rang. This morning when she'd got up she'd turned the volume on the answering-machine up. She was feeling generally more calm and a bit curious to know who was calling. She listened to the message being recorded.

"This is Dr. Adin's office calling again. You missed your appointment yesterday and I'm afraid because you didn't cancel we're going to have to charge you the minimum charge for an examination. Since I haven't been able to reach you, you need to call and confirm your next appointment, Monday, April 18 at 10:00 a.m. Otherwise I'll have to consider it cancelled."

Margaret's sense of well-being vanished. She realized she didn't even know what day it was or what week. The phone rang again and a bank clerk left a message telling her she'd missed a mortgage payment and needed to make arrangements to pay it immediately. A few minutes later John phoned and left a brusque message to call him back.

The bank wouldn't have called John. After they got married they'd continued the financial arrangement they'd had when they lived together: separate bank accounts and a joint account to which they contributed equally for living expenses. Before the wedding Margaret had used a small inheritance from her mother as a down payment on the house, and John paid her half the market value for rent every month. Once he'd started his practice she'd borrowed money from him occasionally to meet her end of the expenses. Legally he was probably entitled to half the house, but they'd been so clear about their fiscal divisions she expected he'd only want her to repay what she'd borrowed. She didn't want to ask for his help now.

From time to time it had occurred to her that their financial arrangement was odd. After they got married they had briefly contemplated pooling their resources and merging possessions. Why hadn't they? She thought it had something to do with her wanting to be independent, wanting to know she was paying her own way. And John had been concerned about the debt he was carrying from medical school and the expense of buying a practice, and he didn't want the burden of underwriting Margaret's sculpture. They both knew that her income as an artist was unlikely to pay for much more than materials, and her other work doing models and replicas for displays wasn't steady. Also he suspected her of being a bit vague when it came to money and thought it was good for her to have to think about it.

"You need to deal with the real world," he said once.

"The real world," she scoffed. "You don't know anything. There is no real world."

She stood unable to move, even to turn the volume back down on the answering-machine, unable to phone the dentist's office, or the bank. Minutes slipped away and she couldn't move to stop them, to mark them with an action, to give them any boundaries, any beginnings or ends. She'd lost her bearings. She no longer knew where she was in time. It was washing over her, carrying her to oblivion and she couldn't move.

A couple of hours passed while she stared at the lighter rectangles on the walls where John had removed paintings, or at the indentations on the carpet from the legs of pieces of furniture he'd taken. Eventually her eyes came to rest on a black book sitting on top of the bookshelf; several minutes later questions formed in her mind. What is that book? What is it doing on top of the bookshelf? I didn't put it there. John must have.

Her curiosity was slight but it was enough to make her go over and pick the book up. It was a Bible that had belonged to her grandmother. John must have started to pack it then realized it was hers and not bothered to put it back on the shelf. A red ribbon marked Psalm 121:

> *I will lift up mine eyes unto the mountains;*
> *From whence shall my help come?*

The psalm they had chosen for their wedding, quite likely still marked from when she and John had looked together. Her mother had told her when she was a girl that it was her grandmother's favourite. During the service she'd lifted her eyes up to the church window. It had been raining lightly and the window was filled with a soft light, a little greyer than her veil and dress. Rivulets of water ran down the pane. She'd trembled. John stood beside her—so erect, noble, self-sufficient. The question echoed inside her, "From whence shall my help come?" and she thought, *Will I need help?* And then she thought, *One looks to mountains because help is such a distant thing.* And then she thought, *I feel safe.*

Was she afraid? She couldn't remember. She remembered trembling, feeling dizzy, being too overwhelmed to feel anything distinctly.

But wasn't it natural to be afraid on one's wedding day?

> *He will not suffer thy foot to be moved,*
> *He that keepeth thee will not slumber.*

Her feet were planted so lightly on the ground, as though with one step she would float up into the air and be lost to everyone, sailing up into the infinite soft clouds and—to prevent this—a man who never slept and was as immovable as the trunk of a tree, who would hold her feet to the ground in place beside him.

> *The sun shall not smite thee by day,*
> *Nor the moon by night.*

She saw herself as a pretty anxious person but it never would have occurred to her that the sun itself might strike her down, where she stood, or that the moon, the beautiful, cool, white moon, might strike her down too. How had she overlooked this promise of protection against a danger she hadn't even known enough to fear? She'd thought the psalm was about being absolutely protected and guarded by someone who loved you. Now suddenly it seemed more as though the offer of protection had a nasty side.

The minister, pale and serious, intoned the rest of the psalm.

> *The Lord shall keep thee from all evil;*
> *He shall keep thy soul.*

As she whispered the words "I do" to the minister and turned to John, thinking—*Everyone feels like they're marrying a stranger*—even as she swooned at her bridegroom's handsome face, she knew the Lord would not protect her. And she knew she was unprepared to protect herself from the sun or the moon; she could not resist the evil without, much less that within.

The phone rang again. The answering-machine clicked and this time she listened to John's voice repeating their message: "We're not in right now. Leave a message after the tone and we'll get back to you as soon as possible." His voice had a warmth she found surprising, and that made her feel even more desolate.

"Hi. It's me. Helen. Remember me? Haven't heard from you in eons. Did you go on a trip or something? Call, if just to say you're still alive."

The machine rewound the outgoing message. The red light blinked.

What if John was a warm, loving man and it was really she who was unfeeling and self-absorbed? Had she ever desired him, or had she only wanted to be desired? This wasn't the first time she'd wondered. Had she ever wanted to take him or had she only wanted to be taken? Was this why John had become so uninterested in sex? Had he sensed that she didn't desire him, but was possessed only by an insatiable need to be the object of his desire? Had he sensed that he was being cast not entirely in the role of lover but also of pain-reliever?

Vanity. All is vanity, Ecclesiastes echoed.

She had conducted an experiment. She had tried to seduce him. She had simulated desire, hoping that might lead her to actually experience it. As he lay on his back, naked, ready to sleep, she probed his mouth with her tongue. She kissed his chest, his testicles, took his penis into her mouth. Tried to bring him to orgasm, to enjoy doing so for its own sake. But his erection softened. *He senses a fake,* she thought.

She felt her humiliation physically. She had not

known what to do with her body, her limbs, how to arrange her face. Every part of her felt bluntly rejected.

They pretended that he was overtired from work and said goodnight with affectionate smiles. But as soon as the lights were out, she turned to the wall and made sure no part of her was touching him. She listened to his breathing, first as he feigned sleep, then as he fell into real sleep. She tried to repair her sense of humiliation by raging at him, by feeling sorry for herself, by thinking of him as cruel and cold. Then by vacating her body.

Now her heart was pounding yet her blood felt thick and slow. She was anxious yet overcome with lethargy and weariness. The effort to survive was too great. She was going to miss the mortgage payment. Property tax was overdue. And now she owed money to the dentist for work that hadn't even been done. She wasn't going to get paid for her last job because she was incompetent. She felt like an animal in the wild who doesn't have the wit or energy to gather food, let alone anticipate the need to protect itself from predators. Doomed to die while other creatures or species flourished.

"In sickness and in health. Till death do us part."

I made vows, Margaret thought.

She could not have promised more, could not have vowed with more conviction than she had on her wedding day, despite her fear. She *had* thought it was forever. Now, with divorce ahead and a one-night affair behind her, she felt ashamed, unworthy of her vows. Her words meant nothing; they were moths springing from her mouth, unable to hold their meaning from one moment to the next.

A vow bound the present to the future and now she

was cut off from the future, stranded in this present—a silent, empty living room.

The mountain rumbled. Margaret imagined Lucy again, walking, stopping in her path, squinting uncertainly in the direction of Mount Sadiman. The sun glared over the mountain's right shoulder.

The sun shall not smite thee by day...

The ground trembled. Her toes clenched slightly, trying to grip the hard, dry earth.

He will not suffer thy foot to be moved.

Like the passing of a herd of wildebeests. She looked around, eyes wide with alarm. No animal except a bird, flitting from tree to tree.

I will lift up mine eyes unto the mountains;
From whence shall my help come?

TEN

She was sitting in the armchair of her studio reading Neill's notes on the attachment of the temporalis muscle to the skull crest of gorillas, but she was restless and didn't want to read or think any more. She wanted to do something physical, to start a job and finish it, to improve something or fix it, and immediately the rosebush came to mind, out there in her garden struggling under the dead weight of dry branches and the brown shells of last year's rosehips. Forming new rosebuds. She decided to prune it even though it was the wrong season.

Since she'd last been out in the garden the irises had grown tall thick blades which carried blooms furled up inside. Some of the tubers had caved into the large hole she'd left when she dug up the bird's bones and their leaves were turning brown and ragged. She went over and kicked the dirt back in and tamped it around their base with her knuckles. What other bones might lie beneath her garden? What natural wonders might float up from the centre of the earth? Her lilies had sent flower stems up too, and the delphiniums and peonies were bushy and burgeoning.

She got the small pruning saw out of the garage and stood before the rosebush. It looked impregnable and chaotic. She tried to remember the procedure for pruning. Cut away all dead or diseased branches, all branches that cross. Cut above a thorn at an angle leading away from it, since the new growth will sprout from the thorn's saddle near the branch. She should really be wearing heavy gardening gloves, but she didn't have any.

First she lopped off the dried rosehips at the top which was easy, mindless work. Then she cut away the dead branches and the ones whose leaves were spotted with fungus. Finally she tried to determine which was the crossing branch and which the crossed; she pruned slowly, mostly having to make arbitrary decisions about which to remove. Slowly she scattered debris over the lawn and approached the heart of the bush.

There beside four healthy stalks she found two thick dead ones. When she tried to cut them, her thin pruning saw buckled and slipped and its fine teeth could not penetrate more than the outer skin. Three grey stumps at the base of the rosebush were evidence that other gardeners had amputated main stalks. Gardeners with the right tools, something Margaret never seemed to have. Her father had kept their house and garden neat and orderly—how was it that she never noticed what tools he used to achieve this?

She hated to abandon her pruning, but without a

heavier saw she had no choice. Her forearms were quite badly scratched and the thorns' mild poison caused the wounds to welt and sting.

It seemed to her humans might not be as fit for life as rosebushes. Humans must endure unpruned, keeping the wounded and dead parts of themselves with them like tin cans tied to a bumper, clattering and banging, forever getting snagged and tangled in obstructions.

She went back inside the house, leaving the lawn covered with a tangle of pruned branches. She was frustrated at not being able to finish the job. Her head felt full of bees, static electricity and dust; particles festered in crevices and passageways were blocked by dusty piles. She wished she could unscrew it, stick it under the tap and swirl cold water round the inside. She wanted to scrub it out and rinse it and leave it on the dish rack to drain. Screw it back on when it was dry and clean. In its current state she couldn't bear carrying it around much longer. Any minute she'd be forced to take drastic action and she would cry, "Off with my head!" like some masochistic Queen of Hearts.

She tried instead to clear her mind with more physical work and began building a wooden frame for the reconstruction. She nailed an upright post to a wide base and buttressed it at the bottom. She screwed eye hooks into the corners of a rectangle and nailed this on top of the post so she could suspend the skeleton like a marionette and adjust its limbs until she got the posture right. She nailed two poles transversely across the post. These would help support the reconstruction until it was finished and could be properly bolted to the display floor.

ELEVEN

It was hard to imagine how she could feel worse. She'd taken a total of seven 292s in the last ten hours trying to dull the throb of an upper molar toothache, yet they'd barely taken the edge off and now they were making her very nauseous. She'd only slept a couple of hours during the night, and those quite fitfully. And it was her own fault because she'd forgotten her dentist appointment on Monday when the molar would have been filled.

Dr. Matilda Smith was giving a lecture to a crowd of almost a hundred people crammed into a small theatre intended to seat seventy-five. She had large, strong teeth and a robust, capable body, like an English schoolgirl who played a lot of field hockey. She was speaking about her latest find—a female Australopithecus afarensis pelvic bone, tibia, nearly complete skull, a complete humerus and partial ulna and assorted ribs and vertebrae. These fossils were displayed in foam-padded metal boxes on a table beside the podium. The Tanzanian government had granted Dr. Smith permission to travel with them for one year to Canada, the United States and Australia, where she taught university.

Margaret was crumpled up in her chair trying to concentrate but finding that her eyes kept dropping shut, only to pop open again when a fresh wave of nausea swelled inside her, and then she'd breathe in very even, small pants. She would have gone home to bed except that the Chief of Exhibits had arranged for a select group to meet Dr. Smith afterwards and see the fossil bones firsthand. Margaret didn't want to miss the chance to touch the original bones of such an ancient ancestor.

On her way out of the theatre she bumped into Neill chatting with someone near the exit. His tie was an ugly brown-and-maroon colour and it was too short. His shirt was too small and stretched tightly across a soft band of fat she hadn't noticed before. The band of fat forced his blue jeans to ride low but the effect was to make him look relaxed and comfortable rather than slovenly, perhaps because, despite the fat, he was quite muscular. His hair was short and blunt and looked like he'd cut it himself. They shook hands. His gaze moved down to the scratches criss-crossing her forearm, which had welted and reddened and now looked quite dramatic.

"I pruned the rosebush yesterday," she said. He listened to her with a kind of restless perceptiveness.

Neill led the way to the lab where the group was meeting. They came to a flight of stairs leading to the second floor. Margaret had to stop halfway and lean heavily on the banister. The effort to climb was making her heart pound and the increased circulation made the pressure on her tooth unbearable. She felt dizzy. Perspiration broke out on her upper lip. Neill, who'd bounded up to the top, looked back, surprised that she wasn't right behind him.

"I think the 292s are nauseating me," she explained. "I had a toothache all night." Her mouth went from dry to wet to dry to wet. She had to keep swallowing.

He came back down the stairs reluctantly, looking at his watch. "Frank said to be there at twelve-thirty sharp. Dr. Smith only has an hour to spare." He began bobbing from side to side behind Margaret like a sheepdog trying to herd her up the stairs. "It's twelve-thirty now," he said.

"You go ahead." She was too miserable to suppress a certain irritation in her tone. "Just tell me where the washrooms are."

He gave her directions to the washroom and to the lab, then hurried off. She felt she was going to vomit soon so she hobbled as quickly as she could up the stairs, down a hall and around a corner to a door marked with a stick figure in a triangle skirt. She knelt in front of the nearest toilet, repulsed for a moment at having to make contact with a floor possibly spattered with the urine of strangers. Her mouth flooded with saliva first and then she retched and her stomach released its contents.

Afterwards she leaned against the metal divider of the cubicle and enjoyed waves of relief. She felt fragile and warm. She washed her face, rinsed her mouth out and tried to recall Neill's directions. "Turn left at the Neanderthal burial scene. Go past the elevators into the archives."

The museum's corridors were windowless and dark,

and she felt as though she were spelunking, worming her body deeper and deeper. The throb of her tooth came and went like a lighthouse beam. Her arms were itchy where the scratches from the rose thorns were beginning to heal. She felt distant and dreamlike, a bit like Alice in Wonderland, wandering through a strange, narcotic world.

"Turn right at the sabretooth skeleton," Neill had said. She couldn't remember his instructions past that point. Banks of metal drawers that went from floor to ceiling transformed the huge rooms of the archives into a maze, broken open occasionally by long tables on which objects too big to fit in the drawers were stored.

One such object was an enormous saddle-shaped skull with two blunt horns joined in a "V" over the snout. Its shape and shiny hard texture reminded her of those automated horses for children in supermarkets. Her mother had always said yes when she asked to ride them. Margaret had needed help to climb onto them because they were so slippery against the cloth of her tights. Her mother would put the money in, then gaze out at the parking lot while Margaret gripped the saddle-horn. She was sure she would fall off and she didn't know what would happen then, but somehow she thought it might mean she would die. She wished her mother would watch her ride and make it seem fun.

The sound of Neill's voice from further down the corridor caught her attention and as she approached she could distinguish the words.

"I used to dig up arrowheads in the summer along a river near our cottage. Once I actually found a skull which I kept hidden in the attic. Probably it was only a few thousand years old; now I would guess native American but then I thought it was the skull of a prehistoric caveman. I felt as though I'd discovered life from another planet. The great thing is I still have the same feeling of excitement and awe and novelty."

Margaret found it restful listening to conversation without being present. Since vomiting, her toothache had begun to subside a little.

"I still get goosebumps," said Dr. Smith. "It feels very personal to me. I feel myself reaching back to my own origins. Part of the excitement at a dig for me is the sense that I'm uncovering clues to the meaning of my own life. It's a rather shivery sensation."

"Yes! Exactly! That's why this display is so important." Frank spoke with his usual boundless enthusiasm. "Evolution has become our modern creation myth. It's our culture's way of trying to understand our place in the universe, and really that's the most important question for human beings, isn't it? Why are we here, where do we come from, who are we?"

Margaret reached the doorway and entered. She looked immediately for the bones before greeting anyone or introducing herself.

"Margaret! You're suffering from a toothache, we hear," Frank called out. "Would you like to sit down? Are you feeling any better?"

"Yes I am, thanks," she said, and she moved to the table where the bones lay. Neill was holding the skull. Frank introduced her to Dr. Smith and they shook hands. She picked up the pelvis. It was small and cold. It had the texture and mass of carved stone. It was much heavier than bone and didn't seem real, didn't seem as though it had ever supported flesh. She was disappointed. No reverberations. No epiphany. No mystery.

The discovery of the bird bones under the roots of the iris in her own garden had filled her with a greater sense of wonder. Maybe it was like the difference between seeing an animal in the zoo and glimpsing one in the wild. Perhaps Mary Leakey had chosen intentionally to leave the Laetoli footprints in their place, buried under plastic and sand; perhaps she'd wanted to save their mystery. Other paleoanthropologists were indignant because they were in danger of being eroded by tree roots.

I'm so perverse, Margaret thought. *Do I have to make the discovery myself to feel any wonder?* She remembered being in the car with her parents on holidays, looking out the car window at a spectacular sunset, filled with a silent sense of beauty. "Maggie! Look at that sunset," her father would say. "Isn't it a beauty!" And it would be ruined for her. His enthusiasm seemed proprietary to her; it laid claim to the experience. And deflated her. That was something she'd liked about her mother. She never said anything. She gazed quietly at the sunset too and had her own thoughts, but never invaded Margaret's.

Perhaps it was the actual digging up of the bones that interested her, how they were discovered in everyday dust. She wanted that experience for herself—the moment of walking along the ground in Africa and finding a bone belonging to a creature so old and different and yet so connected to her. It would be like finding Eve.

She imagined it might feel like the first time she'd looked at stars after someone told her the universe was infinite. She'd stared for hours trying to comprehend and she'd sorted out in a childlike way that stars had a beginning and an end and so they died but the number of them was infinite and the space they lived in was infinite. Somehow this placing of the finite within the infinite seemed important to her but she didn't know why.

"What was it like," she asked Dr. Smith, "actually finding them?"

"It was very dusty and hot. Before I found them I was thinking about skin cancer. After I found them I couldn't even feel the heat and I thought only that the dust I was breathing might contain molecules of the australopithecine. I hoped the bones would confirm my theory that afarensis still relied heavily on climbing as a mode of locomotion, because the ulna seemed quite long. I wondered why *I* had been given such a gift."

Neill interrupted with a question about some very fine marks on the humerus. He wondered just how strong and robust Dr. Smith thought the creature's arm muscles might have been given the scarring on the bone.

Margaret suddenly didn't care about her own origins or about evolution. She wanted to know who the individual had been. What specific loss was attached to these bones? Who had died?

The bird's skull she'd found under the irises had had a delicate sense of a being still attached to it. Perched in the branches of the fir tree at night. The poignancy of the loss of its individual bird memories and bird attachments.

Lace curtains billowed lightly in moonlight. Outside a single chirp from a sleeping bird. She remembered a hand, Phillip's hand, on her stomach where her flesh was vulnerable, where all the soft organs of digestion and reproduction lay underneath. His hand slowly stroking her belly then resting still as he fell asleep.

For the rest of the hour the group eagerly questioned Dr. Smith about the bones. Margaret thought their hunger for every scrap of information was unseemly and it irritated her. They seemed to be cannibalizing the bones, gnawing on them to fuel a desperate need to feel important, to feel like they belonged in the universe, like they were meant to live—and that they were *evolved.* Margaret decided people's obsession with evolution was narcissistic. No one cared about the creature whose bones these were, what her life had been like except insofar as it told them something about themselves.

She remembered one of Goodall's arguments for the preservation of chimpanzees in the wild. We can learn so much about ourselves from them because they are our closest relatives and that knowledge will be lost to us forever if they become extinct or are reduced to living in zoos or laboratories. The argument had offended Margaret's sensibility—surely the chimpanzees were worth saving in themselves. Yet wasn't there a desperate sadness behind Goodall's argument—wasn't it really a plea? And not just a plea for the preservation of her job?

And these fossil bones everyone in the room was fawning over and revering and turning into fetishes, if they'd belonged to a contemporary creature they would have been tossed casually onto a mountain of other primate bones without so much as a second glance.

The slow strobe of pain had started in her tooth again. Maybe that was the real reason she was so irritated with everyone. Her stomach still felt too fragile and empty for more 292s. She decided to go home, yet she couldn't quite get herself to put the pelvic bone down.

She liked rubbing her thumb over the wide smooth saddle of its cold surface. And she liked its weight in her hand, didn't want her hand to be empty again. She wanted to take it home with her and sit in her armchair and feel its weight in her palm as she looked out the window.

"Margaret, may I see that bone?" Neill asked her.

She looked at him with such raw hostility that the people in the room might have expected to hear a deep growl. She didn't yield the bone right away.

She turned to Dr. Smith. "I'm afraid my tooth has flared up again. You'll have to excuse me." She shook Dr. Smith's hand. "It was a pleasure to meet you."

When had her life stopped? When had it become so flat and limp and paralysed? It was as though she had fallen into a one-dimensional nightmare. She felt like a double-negative imploding on itself. A bundle of spineless vagueness held together by white bandages. Auto-mummification.

TWELVE

She's on an ocean liner in the Antarctic. The ship's bow is like a titanic axe blade of strong narrow steel so it can cut through ice floes. It has just left the dock. Down below whales are swimming around huge chunks of ice. The water is dark green-blue, very dark. It is beautiful standing on deck in the clear sunlight. The whales keep swimming in front of the bow and she's afraid they'll be hit by the sharp steel, but they never are.

Then she's walking down a corridor toward the deck, remembering she has a date to meet Phillip for lunch at an expensive restaurant. The boat, which has just docked, is late and she realizes she can never make it on time. The dock is on the opposite side of town from the restaurant. In fact when she calculates how much time it will take her to get there she realizes she's going to be an hour and a half late. There is so much geography between where she is now and the restaurant where Phillip already waits.

She finds a pay phone on deck and calls Phillip at the restaurant. He answers, "Hello?" He is surrounded by dark wood panelling, heavy burgundy curtains and gold brocade upholstery. Small wall lamps with ivory lampshades envelope him in golden light. She starts explaining that she's going to be late.

"Hello?" he says again. "Hello, hello? Who is this? Hello?"

The phone isn't working. She can hear him but he can't hear her. How can she make him understand she's on her way, that she's not standing him up? She's desperate and yearns to be there. It's only their second or third date. She feels guilty for being late. Why is she so disorganized? Why can't she look at her watch and understand how late it is? *Why can't she manage a simple thing like time?* She is unworthy. He'll wait a while, then leave in disgust. By the time she gets to the restaurant he'll be long gone. She has no way of reaching him after that— she'll never see him again.

She hangs up and starts running in the direction of the restaurant. The streets are crowded. She feels time slipping from her, a nervous jittery feeling in her muscles. More and more people crowd the streets. Lampposts are in her way. Newspaper boxes. Streetlights turn red and cars zoom by in front of her. Her muscles feel as though they are going too slowly, but she can't go any faster. When she tries to speed her legs up it has the opposite effect and slows them down. While she's been worrying, more time has passed.

She knows if she just gave up and relaxed she'd make better time, but she can't help trying.

THIRTEEN

The sound of the dentist's drill was excruciating yet all she felt was a gentle vibration in her skull. For the first time in four days she was completely free of pain. At the bus stop across the street a young woman in torn black jeans smoked nervously. Occasionally she glared around her, defiant yet painfully self-conscious.

Margaret empathized. She herself had basically worn nothing but black from the ages of fifteen to twenty-one. She'd worn it to be inconspicuous, to hide her body. She'd hurried to the back corner seat of the bus, arms crossed over her chest, head down, shoulders hunched, scowling. A thousand times she'd wished she were wearing a bra of cast-iron, a suit of armour, a cloak of invisibility.

Dr. Adin had located the source of her pain in one of the four teeth needing root canals. He'd checked the gums for an abscess and, finding none, opted to take the nerve out that day.

"You won't feel a thing," he'd said when she asked if it would hurt. The long needle felt like a hook piercing her mouth, penetrating right through her jaw. Then the serrated metal of the clamp again. Her gums felt as tender as the soft membrane under the tongue.

But eventually that discomfort subsided and now she lay quite comfortably, oblivious to Dr. Adin poking deeper and deeper into the core of her decayed tooth as he removed all the living tissue.

A pleasant warmth suffused her like the luxurious warmth of bed just before sleep, warmth following the sudden absence of pain. She found the silent, undemanding company of another person comforting.

This silence was short-lived, however, as Dr. Adin was in an ebullient mood. He leaned over, after affixing a different bit in the drill, and asked through the mask covering his mouth, "How are you doing anyway, Margaret?" She blinked up at him over the edge of the rubber dam, wondering how he expected her to overcome all the obstacles to speech he'd stuffed into her mouth. He began drilling, unperturbed by the absence of an answer, and discussed with his assistant what materials he'd be needing during the course of the root canal.

An old man wearing a fishing hat and a beige zip-up jacket bought a newspaper from the box beside the bus stop and sat on the bench not far from the young woman. He put the newspaper down beside him and from his inside jacket pocket took out a pencil and what looked like a horse-racing form. He jotted down some marks with the pencil then leaned back and looked up at the sky, seemingly content with the pleasures of his form and his newspaper, happy to be outdoors. He had a strange familiarity or familiar strangeness about him, she couldn't quite pinpoint it, a kind of momentary perfection.

The telephone rang at the receptionist's desk. "We're quite busy this afternoon," the receptionist said kindly but firmly, "but if you want to come in anyway Dr. Adin can take a quick look." Margaret closed her eyes.

The assistant leaned over her and suctioned out the hole. "I hope you're feeling better than the last time we saw you," Dr. Adin said, continuing the interrupted conversation. She opened her eyes and nodded obediently—a small motion, so as not to upset any of the apparatuses in her mouth.

In fact she did feel better. So much better she wondered if she weren't a bit fickle to be already recovering from the end of a ten-year marriage. She hadn't thought about John for days. Of course the toothache had consumed most of her consciousness, but also she'd been occupied with reading about Lucy and doing research for the reconstruction.

She'd reread a book by the paleoanthropologist who'd discovered the Lucy skeleton. The first time she'd read this book she'd been completely caught up by the author's excitement. She'd been interested to discover that the ability to walk erect had evolved before a bigger brain, and that it was our bodies, not our brains, that precipitated our humanness.

But this reading of the book was frustrating her. The narrative seemed obtusely to withhold what she most wanted to know. What had Lucy been like? What had she seen, smelled, heard, experienced? What had she felt? What might have happened to her during her life? With a brain only slightly larger than a chimpanzee's, what did she perceive?

Dr. Adin removed the last few objects from Margaret's mouth, stood back and indicated that she should spit into the small circular sink beside the chair. A few brown particles and dark blood appeared fleetingly in the sink before spiralling down the drain.

Margaret told him she could make bigger payments because she was doing a full-body reconstruction of a human ancestor for a museum.

"What species? I'd be very interested in seeing the teeth," he said.

"I don't have the actual teeth. I only have casts of the original fossils. As much of the fine detail as possible is copied on them but the microscopic wear marks won't be there."

"That's okay. I'd still like to see the casts if I could. I'm interested in the flawed structure of human teeth. Enamel crowded up against enamel with just enough space to trap small food particles but not enough space to easily remove said particles. For most humans early tooth decay is inevitable. Without the intervention of a dentist most people would be toothless by forty. I'd be curious to find out if the flaw in the design was there from the start, or if it only evolved later. What species did you say?"

Margaret promised to bring the casts to one of her next appointments. She waited at the front desk for the receptionist to finish on the telephone. Her jaw was sore from being held open so long.

"How would next Friday be? The twenty-second, four days from now?" the receptionist asked, her tone implying that this appointment should not be forgotten.

Human teeth. The evolution of human teeth. The growing of human teeth. Babies sprouted teeth like razorsharp seedlings out of their tender gums. She thought of the myth of Jason and the Argonauts where teeth were sewn in the earth like seeds. Row upon row of organic warriors.

"Ms. Fisher? The twenty-second?" the receptionist repeated severely.

The only formal claims on her time now were occasional meetings at the museum and there were none scheduled. As she replied that Friday would be fine, something moved in her memory. April 22. What was it? Her parent's wedding anniversary, yes, but that wasn't it. Something else.

"The twenty-second will be fine," she said distractedly, trying to remember why that day was important.

God! Now she remembered. She'd answered the phone. She was hosting a dinner party Friday. She'd completely forgotten. A knock at the door, a peep through the peephole, unlock the door mystified by the unexpected appearance of friends. The totality of her memory lapse startled her. What other commitments might she have made?

When she got home from the dentist she dialled June and David's number. It rang for a long time, then their answering-machine came on the line. She was relieved not to have to speak to them. Now there could be no argument, no cajoling, no questioning. And afterwards she could just turn her machine on and not have to speak to them for days if she didn't want to.

"Hi June, David. I'm afraid I have to postpone dinner this Friday. I'm working on something for the museum that has a very tight deadline and I'll have to pretty much work straight through for the next couple of weeks. How about the twenty-eighth—that's three weeks from now? I'll see if Helen can come too. See you then. Hope you can come. Sorry." And she hung up, pleased to have made her escape so painlessly. Three weeks seemed like a long time away and by then she was sure she'd want to see people again.

The next day at 9:30 in the morning the museum's delivery truck arrived. The driver wheeled in three small and one large wooden crate, asked Margaret to sign for them, then drove away. She got a hammer and pried open the top one, marked "Complete Skeleton A." Inside, wrapped in plastic and protected by foam chips and cardboard, was half a complete skeleton of a female Australopithecus afarensis cast in yellow dental plaster. Another crate marked "Complete Skeleton B" contained the other half.

Neill had gone over the process by which he'd created complete skeletons for the male and female with Margaret. He wanted her to understand each of his decisions in detail. He had used several strategies. First, if a bone existed for one side of the body but not the other, he had used symmetry and constructed a mirror-imaged one for the other side. Then, in cases where a fossil existed for one gender but not the other, he had taken into account the sexual dimorphism in the species and the more gracile aspect of the females. He'd worked back and forth from male to female until he'd filled in all the missing parts that could be taken from the opposite gender. Finally, no complete skull had been found for afarensis, so Neill had had to study the fossils of other species of Australopithecus and rely on his knowledge of comparative anatomy in chimpanzees, gorillas and humans to make a good scientific guess.

The third crate was labelled "Good Cast of Originals—Lucy." Inside was a case very similar to Dr. Smith's containing the museum's display-quality replicas of the Lucy fossils. While the yellow plaster bones hadn't evoked any emotion in Margaret other than a desire to get working on the reconstruction, these fascinated her. She would pick one up, close her eyes and let her hand explore its weight, its volume, its surfaces, its texture over and over. Her fingers tried to imprint into her memory the sensual dimensions of each bone and create a kinesthetic image of it inside her. Hours passed and twilight changed the light in her studio to a soft blue-grey, and still she sat in her armchair, eyes closed, turning one bone, then another, over and over in her hands.

The following day, Wednesday, she arranged to rent an overhead projector. She phoned Frank to see if the museum's truck would be available to pick it up and deliver it to her. John had the car and she wanted to avoid any conversation that might lead to the subject of the division of property. She also opened the fourth large crate. It contained a collection of gorilla, chimpanzee and human bones Neill had sent over for her to use as reference points.

She took a bus downtown and went first to the art supply store and bought a roll of tracing paper, a new sketchpad, sienna ink, umber ink, a new nib for her drawing pen, a huge carton of modelling clay and acrylic paint. At the hardware store she got wire, string, glue for wood, glue for plastic, glue for metal, glue for porcelain (fast and slow-drying varieties), electrical tape, plastic tubing, a heavy pruning saw. She took a taxi home.

New art supplies always made her feel like working. She set the projector up in her studio, tacked tracing paper onto the wall and began the work of projecting onto the paper each yellow dental plaster bone, reduced 25 percent, and tracing its outline. This took the rest of Wednesday and all day Thursday. She went to the dentist Friday morning and in the afternoon began overlaying the tracings of each bone on her drawing table to form a skeleton, taping some down and leaving others loose. To reduce the number of pieces of paper she was working with, she assembled the parts with immobile joints, like the rib cage, and traced them onto one piece of paper.

Once she had the small translucent skeleton assembled she began fiddling, moving arm bones and leg bones into slightly different positions, trying to arrive at a posture consistent with the moment of hesitation in the Laetoli footprints.

None of her arrangements had the subtlety she wanted. As her frustration grew, she ventured less and less realistic poses, creating an increasingly hybrid being, mocking postures from human culture. She drew an apple tree with a snake wound around its trunk and the skeleton picking an apple from its branches. She drew a martini glass and made it sip a martini. She drew a handsome suitor and made the skeleton push him away.

At around ten o'clock she decided to abandon the

skeleton and try sketching Lucy first. If she produced a drawing she liked she could arrange the traced bones to match it. She set out photographs of chimpanzees, gorillas and humans on her worktable and selected ones that suggested listening. In most of these photographs the subjects had an aspect of alarm or apprehension to them; listening seemed to be defensive.

As Margaret began to draw the creature's listening gestures, she listened to every sound and analysed it. Wind. Raccoon. Man. Outwardly contemplative, inside—anxiously alert.

Though her house was on a pleasant street with a park at the end where old women and men performed Tai Chi in the morning and through which children dawdled on their way to school, after sunset the atmosphere of the neighbourhood changed. The streets echoed with random sounds, tribal hoots from gangs of boys, young females shrieking in terror or nervous exuberance—she'd wait in silence trying to determine which. Heavy-metal blasted from a house down the street, the powerful woofers vibrating neighbours' windows. Glass broke, a gravelly-voiced man shouted at the darkness, looking for a fight. Chinese grandparents stayed inside one another's houses and played mah-jong. Tires screeched. Someone vomited in the alley. An argument between a man and woman escalated to screams, then thumps. A police car drove by silently, toplight flashing.

Alone in the house behind locked and bolted doors, she felt trapped. She felt as though everyone outside knew she was inside and frightened and alone. Like prey waiting for a predator. Since John had gone, she listened more closely to the street. She didn't play music after dark any more because it masked sounds she might need to hear.

There were the police, of course. Over and over she fantasized having to dial 911. She always misdialled—912, 811, 611. The back door was being smashed open. Finally she dialled right and the emergency operator would be asking questions—what was her address? what was wrong?—and she wouldn't be able to answer for fear the intruder would hear her and discover where she was.

But the police, if one had the time to call, took ten to fifteen minutes to arrive. She knew how vulnerable flesh was. They could not reverse wounds, or restore an inviolate vagina, anus, mouth to her. Laws could only punish after the damage was done.

She drew Lucy several times, always gazing into the distance, her head tilted, leaning slightly forward, the small fingers of one hand delicately raised. Margaret took these drawings over to her armchair and sat down and stared at them. She imagined the landscape Lucy might have lived in. Grassy woodland dissolving into savanna, montane forest within sight perhaps. The creature stood far from the shadow of any tree, surrounded by dry yellow grasses. The grass was high—in some places over her head.

She craned her neck, one hand lightly touching the bark of a fallen tree, and listened. Her back was to the woodlands and her skin could sense its cool green shadows. The sun warmed her shoulder and one side of her face. She was still chilled from the cold spring night and she turned toward the sun to absorb more warmth on her chest. Something moved against the wind. Followed by a rustle that was not a breeze.

She froze, listening closely for the next sound. The

hair on the back of her neck and shoulders stood up. She sensed the hushed silence of something else listening too. Her group had found a fig tree twenty or thirty metres away and she could hear their excited exclamations to one another. She knew from their sounds it was full of ripe fruit and she wanted to join them and eat her share, but what she'd heard in the grass stopped her.

A quick stream appeared through the grass flowing directly toward her; she heard panting. She screamed, searching for a tree to climb, looking with brief, doomed comprehension at the woodlands too far away. She had time to hear answering screams from over the rise before the leopard was on her, flying through the air, jaws wide open.

Margaret opened her eyes. Her heart was pounding. Her hand went up to her throat—she could still feel the hot breath from the leopard's mouth. She was momentarily disoriented, thinking she was surrounded by tall grass. She was very relieved when she realized she was in her house, in a city, with paved roads and suburbs and industrial parks between her and wild animals.

In her research she'd read about the skull of a juvenile Australopithecus robustus, an extinct vegetarian branch of the hominid tree, whose cranium was pierced by two holes. The holes were later matched to the lower canines of a fossilized leopard jaw. Australopithecines had been part of the food chain, preyed upon like deer or pigs. Packs of hyenas had yelped at the heels of lions and leopards, waiting to scavenge the small curled-up carcasses, their ghosts given up.

FOURTEEN

She sat on the back step feeding the tuna-fish out of her sandwich to a neighbourhood cat. It was the one she liked most, a calico cat that seemed deliriously happy just to be alive. It often performed death-defying gymnastics in the morning sunlight as it sought to catch bugs out of the air. It was able to create suspense any-where, anytime, by suddenly crouching low or whirling round and snapping at the air.

It licked her finger with its rough pink tongue. It had black lips and needly sharp white teeth. Margaret remembered the leopard flying at her throat through the air, its hot breath exuding the smell of digested raw meat.

No wonder people love cats. The transmogrification of a mortal enemy into a pet. We like to do that to our enemies. Bring them into our living rooms, feed them, pet them, keep an eye on them, reassure ourselves over and over again that they cannot hurt us. Part of the pleasure in going to the zoo is seeing our predators in cages.

The cat looked for more tuna-fish. Margaret put the bread face-up on the steps, thinking the cat might want to lick the remnants of fish off, but a bee flew by and the cat's head turned to watch. It readied itself to leap, drawing its hind legs in closer underneath and growing still. The bee flew into one of the bell-shaped flowers of a foxglove and the tension in the cat dissolved. It trotted over to the flower and sat looking up at it for a while, then got distracted and walked down the garden path into the back alley.

It occurred to her that after the wedding, when she'd realized John was a stranger to her, she'd tried to do that to him—domesticate him so she could feel sure he wasn't an enemy. A husband was too close, too hard to defend against should he prove hostile.

And she felt unsure that he wasn't hostile, that he didn't, in some petty way at least, wish her harm. No, that wasn't fair, not wish her harm so much as remain indifferent should harm come to her while he was pursuing his own desires.

She remembered not wanting him to go out with a particular group of male friends who were loud, boisterous—disloyal to women. She subtly tried to express disdain for them, but John had a radar for any encroachments on his freedom. "They're not perfect like your friends," he'd said sarcastically, "but they're good guys and I've known them since high school." After that every time he went out with them the air was charged. She retreated to her studio and waited for him to go, calling, "Bye dear," as she heard the front door open, or she tried to go out herself, just to get away from the weight of the conversation that was going unsaid.

Only a sure hand can succeed at manipulation. The person must feel they're in the hands of a master, and though Margaret was someone who wanted control very much, her attempts were transparent and ineffectual.

John would go through TV-watching jags when he was depressed. He watched sports: baseball, football, hockey, golf, tennis, boxing; any sitcoms or comedy shows; any cop shows. She understood that he just wanted to lose himself in the contained narratives of games and jokes, but she couldn't stand the canned laughter and the calculated hushes and crescendos of sports commentary blaring through the house for the whole day.

She'd walk into the living room, John would glance up, then look back at the screen, and she'd gaze at the screen too for a minute or two. Then she'd say in a false conversational tone, "It's a beautiful day outside," or "Boy, the grass is getting long in our yard," or "Did you read that book I gave you last week, the one about black holes?" He'd answer monosyllabically, "Oh," or "Mmm" or "No," and suddenly get intensely interested in something happening on the screen.

She'd spend the rest of the afternoon compulsively fantasizing about marching back into the living room, ripping the plug out of the wall, carrying the television outside to the front porch and smashing it on the sidewalk. The imagined sound of exploding tubes and breaking glass, and the ensuing peace, were richly satisfying. But they'd just have to buy another TV. And if John was depressed why shouldn't he drown himself in

TV? Why couldn't she just leave him be?

Her efforts at control—domestication—only resulted in increased tension.

She picked the bread up from the step and threw it into the garbage can on the porch. Had she domesticated herself instead? Was that why she didn't feel fully alive?

Over the next week she attached the yellow plaster bones to each other with different thicknesses of wire. She followed Neill's notes and the work went quickly. The skeleton began to have a presence that was not wholly inanimate; it evoked the kinesthetic sense of an impending body, it telegraphed motion. She was beginning to visualize flesh on the bones, to imagine how the reconstruction would look when it was finished.

She attached the skull last. It was the heaviest and the hardest to stabilize. She wanted it at an angle, tilted to the left and slightly forward. An ear to the ground. Cocked robin. She used the heaviest wire she had but even so, with the slightest touch, the skull sank down or bent way back. So she got a metal bar, inserted it through the spinal corridor of the cervical vertibrae and up through a small hole she'd drilled in the foramen magnum of the skull. She bolted it in place.

Phillip's head was heavy. It looked as though it would take very strong neck muscles to keep it from falling over, yet Phillip's neck didn't seem unusually strong. The heaviness of his head combined with his curly grey hair had made his head seem leonine, and yet his neck seemed almost fragile by comparison, poetic. She'd wanted to take the weight of that great lion head in her hands, just to feel its volume.

She took her sketches of Lucy over to the armchair and sat down to analyse whether the yellow skeleton was assembled in the right posture to recreate a sense of intense listening. Today was the last day she could easily change it because tomorrow, after she'd attached the jawbone, she would fuse all the joints with glue so the skeleton would not shift when she began putting on flesh.

She felt restless and checked her watch. The eleven o'clock news had just started. She made some mint tea and went into the living room to watch it. The news announcer's stock facial expression had a trace of regret and he spoke in a slightly hushed tone.

"We're sad to announce that only two hours ago the new baby killer whale at the aquarium passed away." The screen cut to the head and shoulders of a woman in a wet suit. "Trainer Vicky Hillsborough is one of many at the aquarium who are mourning the loss of the spunky little whale."

"It probably died of starvation," the trainer said, looking tired and defeated. "For the last few days it seemed to be having trouble getting enough milk from the mother." Back to the announcer.

"Ian McDougall, a marine biologist at the aquarium, said that even in the wild the mortality rate for baby whales is quite high, and marine biologists do not yet understand all the causes for their deaths. The staff at the aquarium decided not to name the little whale because they were concerned right from the start about its chances for survival. They didn't want the children who visit the aquarium to become too attached to it until they knew if it would make it."

Last week they had shown the baby's body being

expelled by the mother whale's vagina amid milky wisps and clouds, then the baby swam around and around, like a giant overjoyed minnow. A few days later they'd shown it nuzzling its mother's belly, and the mother nosing it affectionately. Yesterday there was footage of it swimming listlessly. It had stopped gaining weight. The aquarium staff didn't know if the mother wasn't producing enough milk, or if the baby had no appetite because it was sick. No one seemed to be able to do anything for it, which was surprising to Margaret.

She went into the studio and turned out the lights before going to bed. Moonlight shone in across the back alley, making the bright mustard-yellow of the dental plaster look a dark blue-grey. It caused deep shadows in the orbits of the eyes and Margaret's gaze was drawn to the rich blackness of these shadows. Her fingers ran along the supraorbital ridge under her own eyebrow and she felt the deep curve inward of the sockets. She'd never really thought about there being a skull under her face before, never wondered what that skull looked like.

Margaret envisioned Lucy's eyes, just the eyes, looking through time, blazing with pain and sadness, and then she saw her own skull, cleaned of flesh, overlaid on Lucy's face. The room had an aura of fullness, of fertilized empty space. For the first time in three years Margaret felt an idea forming for a sculpture, a kind of inchoate nagging to excavate an image from a piece of stone. Who was it? What was this form calling from the dark orbital caves, not yet come into the light? Eyes staring at her, bone structure floating, circling. What other self calling across the debris of millenniums? Who is it?

Margaret woke up feeling off-kilter, wobbly in her thoughts, airy, uneasy and a bit choked-up. There was a small knot in the back of her throat that ached, the way it did sometimes just before she cried. She made coffee and went right to her studio.

She backed right off the idea of sculpture. She wasn't ready yet to tackle that aspect of her life. She wasn't ready to deal with the disappointment if she ended up shaping a lump of stone with no tension, no kinetic energy, no beauty. Just a dead, worthless lump of stone.

She lifted the lower jawbone from its foam bed in the crate. Embedded in the garish yellow plaster were realistic-looking teeth. The enamel was stained brown and the back molars were quite worn down.

The only aspect of the jaw that was human was the small size of the canines. The dental arcade was V-shaped and quite unlike the box-like configuration of a chimpanzee, or the U-shaped one of humans and other australopithecines. The molars seemed enormous for such a tiny mouth.

Margaret began wiring the lower jaw in place, leaving the teeth slightly parted, the chalky taste of volcanic ash in its bony mouth.

She had gorilla, chimpanzee and human female skulls on her worktable along with the replica jawbone and pieces of skull from the Lucy skeleton. Neill's notes described scarring on the frontal and parietal bones of other larger afarensis fossil skulls, indicating the attachment of a very large, powerful chewing muscle. This, along with the broad, somewhat flat molars and the microscopic wear marks examined on original fossil teeth, suggested a primarily vegetarian diet for afarensis similar to that of chimpanzees. Australopithecus afarensis may have killed and eaten small rodents, monkeys, etc., but probably as sporadically as a chimpanzee. A female would have eaten only the scraps she could beg or steal.

She imagined Lucy breaking a piece of bark from a rotten log. Underneath fat white grubs twinkled against the red wood. She quickly plucked one up and put it in her mouth. She concentrated fiercely, not wanting to miss any.

Margaret decided to take a break before starting to fuse all the joints with glue. She went out into the garden, feeling at loose ends and melancholy. She should do something to change her mood, she thought, something that required physical exertion. Three years ago she'd planned to dig a round bed by the back fence where it got a lot of sun and would be perfect for tomatoes. She knew it was three years ago because John's sister and brother-in-law had been visiting. John's sister had been six months pregnant and she and her husband were very gay together, laughing and hugging and teasing. That was when Margaret noticed she and John had stopped touching each other, and even really stopped speaking except out of necessity or courtesy. After that, homegrown tomatoes had stopped seeming particularly desirable. She no longer really cared whether she ate tasteless mushy ones that came up in refrigerated trucks from California.

The spade was in the garage behind a cracked and brittle plastic garden hose. She positioned the spade where she thought the edge of the bed should be and pushed down with her foot. It barely penetrated. She pushed harder, with no result. She stood on the spade with both feet and jumped up and down, like a beginner on a pogo-stick. The matted web of grass and roots still resisted.

She found she had to pry the turf up in very small pieces at first. Then she could manage bigger chunks, which looked like giant toupees. She shook them to loosen clumps of dirt and worms hanging among the roots.

Once the bed was dug she sifted through the earth, removing pieces of weed and the knotted webs of root systems. She found an old soggy cardboard box, turquoise like Birk's jewellery boxes. The bottom and lid had been fused together by moisture from the earth. She peeled back the top and inside was a small green turtle shell with bits of things—dirt, turtle flesh perhaps, flakes of turtle skin and particles of turtle nails and turtle bones—all almost turned to earth.

Some of the scales were flaking off the shell. On the underside, a striking brown pattern, like a drawing of the tree of life, was still evident. The empty holes where the legs had been made her a little squeamish, bringing to mind the poor leathery limbs that would have been there, struggling to get away from her had the creature been alive. She laid the box aside on the lawn.

By the time she'd finished perfecting the curve of the new bed's circumference, the sun was illuminating clouds from below, igniting their underbellies to a brilliant orangey-pink. The garden had cooled in the evening's shadows and everything was tinged with blue. The street was quiet; people were inside eating dinner. She felt purged and light with sadness, as though she might float over the cool blue grass and vanish into the shadows of the hydrangea.

She remembered driving home one evening last summer with the radio on full blast. A song came on that she loved. The sound was slightly surreal, heavily synthesized, but lyrical, and it delivered a big emotional release for her. She felt suddenly expansive and free and filled with compassion. She knew John liked this song too and wondered then for the first time what their marriage must be like for John and thought it must be painful for him too. She felt a wave of affection for him and new hope infused her. If she walked into their house, hugged him and told him she loved him, wasn't it possible that all the silence and emptiness would melt away? The announcer supplied the name of the group, Soft Cell, but she missed the song title. "Take your hand off me" was the only line she remembered from the chorus.

But when she'd walked in their front door the weight had hit her right away. There'd be no digging themselves out of this black hole. It was too late for that kind of hope.

Though the sun hadn't quite set, a full moon hung in the sky and its cool light competed briefly with the sun's. She lay on the ground by the new bed, sifting the soil absently, gently through her fingers.

She rolled over the lifted the turtle shell out of the box again. This time a small white object gleamed faintly in a soggy corner. It was a tooth. A baby tooth, with bumpy ridges still across the edge. A child wanting to bury a piece of herself with its dead pet turtle.

Margaret held the tooth in her fist and lay back on the grass. The cool blades made goosebumps rise on the back of her arms. The first evening stars were visible.

She thought about the baby whale. They hadn't

named it because they didn't want children to get too attached to something that was just going to die.

But that's what love always is, Margaret thought. Getting attached to something that is just going to die.

FIFTEEN

During the night she woke up sobbing. Sobbing! How dramatic. It sounded so alarming to wake up sobbing in one's sleep. So unbalanced. She had no idea why she was crying—which was also alarming. The sobbing stopped and she went back to sleep. In the morning she woke up feeling as though she were in an unfamiliar world. Sound waves bounced off everything with a flat, one-dimensional tone.

She got up and put on a muu-muu her great-aunt had brought back from Hawaii and handed down to her, saying it was too bright for her old face and it would look much better on Margaret. The print was large sunflowers splashed across a bright blue background. She put on socks and loafers. The unreal feeling persisted.

Each movement she made carried a slight echo, as though her skeleton had a blurred double wavering just apart from her own. Her head felt a foot lower than usual, and when she walked downstairs she had the sensation of having to negotiate each stair carefully because her feet were large and floppy. She wondered vaguely if she were coming down with one of those strange new viruses she occasionally read about in the newspapers.

She felt fine again, though, as she ate breakfast and brushed and flossed her teeth. She packed the casts of Lucy's original jawbones back into the crate they'd arrived in and called a taxi. The driver asked about the crate.

"A bit early for cherries," he said.

"Bones," she answered. She hated talking to taxi drivers. She felt uncomfortable being inside a car—such an intimate, claustrophobic environment—with a stranger. She preferred not to talk.

"Bones!" he exclaimed. Now he was curious.

Margaret never had the courage to just say she didn't want to talk. Instead she gave dull, monosyllabic answers, thinking this would indicate she didn't want a conversation. It never worked.

"What kind of bones?"

Humans were fascinated by bones, she thought. Not bones on a dinner plate, thrown into the garbage without a second thought, the meat gnawed off. But put bones in a box, bury them, assemble them, fossilize them, and they fascinate us.

"Oh, chimpanzee bones," she said, hoping improbably that that would put him off. She really did not want to talk and there was no short explanation for the Lucy casts.

"What do you want them for?"

"I found them in my garden. I think it was murdered."

"What makes you think that?"

"When I dug them up there was a knife embedded in the rib cage," Margaret answered. The driver stopped behind another car at a red light. She turned around and looked out the back window, hoping this might end the conversation. The car behind was an old blue Ford with a cracked windshield. An obese young woman was eating a chocolate bar and a tall thin man, his face gaunt and drawn, gripped the steering wheel. The woman offered him a bite of her chocolate bar—there seemed to be a quality of pleading in her offer—*save me from myself*—but the man shook his head and continued to stare at the traffic light.

> *Jack Sprat could eat no fat*
> *His wife could eat no lean*
> *And betwixt them both*
> *They licked the platter clean oh*
> *They licked the platter clean.*

The woman looked down at the chocolate bar with momentary bewilderment, then defiantly took another bite—*there, now see what you've done.* She seemed angry with him. He had declined to save her from herself, had refused to take her poison into his own body.

The cab stopped in front of the dentist's office and the driver sullenly took her money. He'd had time to think about the murdered chimpanzee story. He seemed to realize she'd been having him on and he bristled with resentment. Margaret felt guilty. She should have been direct with him, like Lucy. Hooted and screamed or snarled till he shut up. She hated being such a coward.

Another patient was still in Dr. Adin's chair, submitting himself to the invasion of metal. Vivaldi was playing over the office speakers, and though beautiful, it did nothing to drown out the squeal of the drill. Margaret thought this was definitely the time and place for heavy rock 'n' roll. Sex Pistols, The Clash, Guns N' Roses, U2, Nirvana, Led Zeppelin. Metal on metal. Dr. Adin's room seemed a cold place full of sharp objects. It made her veins ache.

She'd always felt nervous around sharp objects. Broken glass. Knives. Razor blades. In the same way some people, when standing near the edge of a cliff, had to fight an urge to throw themselves off, had to exert willpower over their leg muscles so they wouldn't step over, Margaret had to fight an urge to slit her wrists, or disembowel herself. Perhaps the urge to do oneself in was quite common. Perhaps a samurai, preparing for hara-kiri, had spent a lifetime resisting just such urges.

Margaret sat down in the waiting room and flipped through a celebrity magazine. Beautiful faces fell quickly on top of one another. She looked closely at some of the pictures and decided that most of the celebrities were actually not that beautiful. Most of them had no taste in clothes and their faces had a kind of worn, gaudy look.

She thought death might be a pleasant release, a deep, warm sleep, the way she felt after an anaesthetic before the nauseating effort to swim up to consciousness. Timeless—"Oh, the operation is over. That's funny, I don't feel different." Warm and safe, down you go.

She thought of her mother and looked quickly out the window, flinching. When her mother had been a young woman she'd tried to kill herself. Had felt that unhappy and weary... The diva's warm operatic voice floating through the house from the hi-fi speakers, a house she shared with another student who was away for the weekend with her fiancé. The bathroom door was ajar upstairs, her mother in the bathtub, tired of dates with young men, all pleasant enough, with their little packages of ambition, of which she, with her voluptuous curves and soft brown eyes, was part and parcel, the pressure of their need—can I do this to you, can I touch here, and here, will you meet my parents, let's go dancing with so and so—the weight of knowing she was nothing, worthless, worse than nothing perhaps by seeming, however unintentionally, to be something. Seeking warm release. Lying in that bathtub, the shabby old terrycloth bathrobe she'd had since she was twelve draped across the chair and the sharp kitchen knife on a stool beside the bathtub, listening in wonder to the voice of Maria Callas floating upstairs, she was ready to let go, to let her blood leak out in swirling cloudy red, but she preferred to anticipate it in black and white because she had not wanted to think of it as blood, just as clouds, like milk in water, making wondrous liquid patterns and shapes, and then there was someone knocking at her front door.

She didn't answer, thinking whoever it was would think no one was home and leave, but the knocking persisted, got louder, and vaguely, thickly, it occurred to her that whoever it was could hear Callas's voice too and knew she was at home.

Margaret knew this story about her mother from her father, who had been the man at the door. He had already started breaking the door down with his shoulder when her mother pulled herself out of the bath, put on her old robe, hid the knife under the bathtub and called down, "Stop, stop, I'm coming." She'd opened the door dripping wet explaining she hadn't been able to hear his knocking over the music.

Her father had been just a little smarter than the rest, pushier, hungrier perhaps, and he'd managed to get her mother pregnant with Margaret. Her birth closed the door on that particular escape route.

Margaret started to weep and hurried to the washroom. Why remember this now? She dried her eyes and blew her nose only to start crying again when she went to pee. It hurt knowing her mother had felt so empty and alone, and that her conception had occurred amid such unhappiness. She needed to stop crying. Cold water. When she was a girl her mother had told her splashing cold water on your face helped stop crying and she'd wondered why anyone who was sad enough to cry would care whether they stopped or not.

On her way back down the hall to the dentist's office, she wondered whether Lucy cried. She didn't think so. When did crying first appear? Why had natural selection favoured it? Did it startle predators? Or did it make aggressors of the same species back off, thus giving an advantage within the species?

Margaret was called into Dr. Adin's office and she carried the crate in with her and put it down in the corner. He ushered her into the chair. She sighed as he tilted her back. She liked this aspect of visiting the dentist, the surrender of control for an hour or so, being powerless, not responsible.

"I brought the casts." She pointed to the crate. Dr.

Adin injected freezing into her gum, then closed the door conspiratorily and brought the crate over to Margaret. She took off the lid and then the layer of foam and handed the lower jawbone to him.

"Be very careful with it. I'm sure you know, but..."

"Of course. The molars are large. And on the premolars there's no metaconid to speak of, just this faint beginning." He pointed to a tiny swelling across the single large cusp on the molar. "Not a bicuspid. There is a marked diastema, obviously had larger upper canines. Do you have an example of those?"

"Not for Lucy. There are several other ones at the museum."

"Same number of teeth but more space than the human jaw. What's most interesting to me, though, is that there's still a fair bit of crowding between the molars. See how they're right up against each other? These creatures would have suffered from some tooth decay. The design was imperfect right from the beginning."

Margaret silently agreed that human teeth were a defective design.

"I don't see any signs of widespread decay. Whoever made the cast did reproduce one caries, however." He drew her attention to a small recess in one of the molars near where the gum line would have been. "That would eventually have caused a howl of pain... How old was Lucy? I see her wisdom teeth have erupted."

"Mid to late twenties."

"In the Middle Ages even teenagers were usually already missing several teeth and showing extensive decay in the back molars. There's an interesting question for research—how much is diet and how much is structure?

You could study patterns of decay in our ancestors and place that in the context of their dental structure and their eating habits and then compare to today…"

He was preoccupied now, his mind racing with the implications of Lucy's teeth.

"Thank you for letting me see this," he said and handed the lower jaw back to her. She placed it in the crate and he carried the crate over to the corner again.

"I think I'll apply for a research grant." He pulled his hygienic mask over his mouth. His eyes twinkled happily down at her from behind his glasses. She sighed again and closed her eyes.

In the taxi on the way home, when the new driver started winding himself up for a conversation, she said she was sorry but she needed to think about something during the drive. She derided herself for using the word "need," with its false suggestion of urgency. "Want" should have been good enough.

It started to rain. She listened to the slick of wheels on the road.

When she unlocked the front door of her home and went inside, the emptiness was resonant. It enveloped her. For a moment she had an impulse to phone John, ask him to come back. It was the same feeling that she had around knives, the edge of release, surrender to doom, wanting to give in to a desire for self-obliteration. "John, please come over right away. I can't bear the sound of my own footsteps. I'm afraid to move because then I'll hear them again. Save me."

"It's all right," she told herself calmly. "You can go over to the couch, sit down and lift your feet off the floor. Then there will be no footsteps. You're not a little girl. You're a grown woman. Nothing's going to happen to you."

She made it to the couch, lay down and drew a blanket over her. The rain stopped. Clouds sailed by on blasts of wind.

"Liar," she replied to herself sarcastically. "*Nothing's going to happen to you!* You don't know that. You're trying to trick yourself. Not only *is* something going to happen, it's going to happen soon, it's inevitable and it's like your worst nightmare.

"Before long, your face, that surface to which you have become so attached, will be a skull. Your lips, for example, will depart from your coffin in the stomachs of maggots. The bands of underlying muscle will exist only as molecules in their faeces. This interconnected intricate system—tendons, ligaments, attaching everything to your bones, arteries carrying food to all the body's cells and the heart that circulates that food, the stomach that translates food into blood, and the mouth that chews and swallows and the hand that feeds the mouth and the eyes that find the food: the whole house of cards will collapse and turn into dust.

"*Nothing's going to happen to you.* Ha! A house of cards in a very gusty place. No wonder you're terrified. Who wouldn't be? To realize one's precious self is merely fertilizer out on a day pass. The strange thing is how everyone else appears to be just getting on with their lives.

"The strange thing is that you thought John could save you."

The voice of a little girl answered petulantly: "I could let him worry about it for a while. If I knew he was thinking about it, I could relax for a while. Take a break. Let him handle it."

"Aha," the skull said. "See what you did to him! You tried to set him up to do battle with *your* demons, so you could eat chocolate-covered cherries and watch TV while he fought to the death. No wonder he balked. He was smart enough to look over his shoulder and there you were, lazing around. That's when he dropped the sword, turned his back on your howling furies and walked away. Meanwhile you'd let yourself get soft and stupid. You were unprepared to face your demons, who were now bent on tearing you limb from limb. The TV kept yapping away but you were too terrified to gain any comfort from it."

"So what did John get out of it?" her detached self asked. "Why did he bother in the first place?"

Maybe my demons were almost identical to his. He could face mine, knowing if things got rough and he started to lose, they'd go after me, not him. Yet if he vanquished them, he would know he stood a good chance of vanquishing his own.

She moaned on the couch. Fiery-eyed masks with sharp hyena jaws snapping, saliva dripping down onto the curved claws of their scaly feet, their dirty wings beating, preparing to swoop down on her.

"What choice do you have?" asked the skull.

"Unhhhh," she moaned. "I could just let them devour me," said the chocolate-eating slut. "Then there'd be nothing for them to get their forked tails all worked up about. I could watch TV in peace."

Lucy came out into the arena. Amid the cacophony she sniffed the air and looked up at the sky, then ambled over to Margaret on the couch and put her long arm round her shoulder. None of Margaret's screaming voices seemed to disturb her. They were a mildly interesting distraction.

Margaret felt Lucy's strong hand pat her shoulder kindly and she relaxed. The furies subsided. She wasn't going to die just this minute. She drifted asleep, dimly aware of the presence in the studio of the reconstruction, the casts of Lucy's bones and an untouched chunk of black marble that seemed to be calling to them.

SIXTEEN

Dust into dust, nothing into nothing. All *is* vanity.
Dust could inhabit the corners of a house for an
eternity, outlasting all other occupants. Margaret
thought of dust as a kind of first particle of matter.
There before the Big Bang, there before the first life
form, and there after the last one. She respected dust.

Even so, she had not taken into account how much
of it she'd let accumulate inside her house. Friday morning, when she thought about cleaning up a little for the
dinner party on Saturday, it was as though a veil was lifted from her eyes. There was dust everywhere. A river of it
flowed through her house, leaving eddies here and there
mixed with strands of hair, crumbs and dead insects.
The ceilings were festooned with spider webs, themselves strung with the shells of dead insects. Window
sills provided soft beds of dust for the desiccated bodies

of flies and bees who'd escaped the webs.

And it wasn't just dust. All the furniture, the carpet and walls were stained and grimy. The bathroom smelled of urine and mildew. The fridge smelled of rotting food and at the bottom, under the crisper drawers, water had collected from the malfunctioning defroster and grown red slime. Whenever she used the stove she had to turn the overhead fan on because all the burners and the oven smoked from spilled food. She checked the back of the freezer to see if something was blocking the little hose where moisture was supposed to trickle out and discovered a stash of individually wrapped pieces of wedding cake from ten years ago. Who had she thought she was going to bless with these precious morsels? Her house was an undisturbed archaeological record of domestic decay.

Before they got married John used to delight in teasing Margaret about her slovenliness. At dinner parties he would recount an anecdote from their early courtship to their friends. "She invited me in for a drink. Naturally I was curious what her place was like because I was in love with her. When I walked in I thought to myself, this woman has real strength of character. She'd made no effort to impress me and seemed utterly unconcerned what I might think. No apologies even."

"What he didn't know," Margaret would add "is I'd spent the whole day cleaning! I *was* trying to impress him."

"How high do you think the dust would be on top of the fridge now if you hadn't met me?"

At first John did all the housework. He would start cleaning and before long, maybe half an hour, he would call her in from her studio to witness the degradation to which she was subjecting their home. "You don't care what happens to this place," he'd say indignantly.

Margaret picked up a huge pile of newspapers from the floor beside the couch and dust exploded, scintillating and unexpectedly beautiful as it spun up and circled her head in the sunlight. Tiny particles floated into her ears and stuck to her hair and eyelashes. She sneezed and watched as specks very indirectly and gradually floated back down to the floor, a universe in each. And conversely a nothingness in the enormous universe.

John was wrong. It wasn't that she didn't care. Actually she liked cleaning the house. The problem was once she started she didn't want to stop. One area of dirt or disorder led to another and another and another. By the time she'd cleaned everything she wanted to clean and organized everything she wanted to organize, the first things she'd cleaned would be dirty again. She'd never have time to do anything else. If only house-cleaning were the kind of job you could finish, if it would stay done even for a week . . . What she couldn't bear was the open-endedness of it, the never arriving, the constant resistance to control. And then when you did arrive finally at the grave, you only created more dust.

Dust was infinite and eternal. Why not just accept the inevitable? Dust into dust. All housekeeping was vanity.

When she quoted Ecclesiastes to her husband to back up her claim that housekeeping was a waste of time, he looked alarmed.

I looked on all the works that my hands had
wrought, and on the labour that I had laboured

*to do: and, behold, all was vanity and vexation
of spirit and* there was *no profit under the sun.*

She had wanted to be taken care of. When she married
John she hadn't wanted adventure or romance, though
she thought she had. All she'd really wanted was security—to return to the womb—and now her house looked
as though it had become some kind of womb or cocoon,
spun with dust and cobwebs and old paper, only small
cubbyholes and passageways free of clutter for the occu-
pant to walk and sit. It looked as though its mistress had
retreated to the centre and folded into a foetal position.

She put the newspapers out on the back porch. She
ran a basin of warm soapy water and carried it into her
study. The tiny bird's skull she'd dug up out of her garden was on the bookcase. She picked it up and dry dirt
sifted out onto the floor. A spider had spun a web
between it and a vase of dried roses, but the web was
empty. Margaret looked inside the bird's skull and saw
the spider, legs curled into its centre, dead.

She considered the spider's lot. It could only weave its
web and wait for the universe to send a fly its way. The
spider could wait a long time, but not forever. If the
universe did not send a fly, something, after weeks or
even years of spider-praying and spider-suffering, the
creature folded up its legs and died. It would have done
all the work set out for spiders to do that they should
live, and still it would starve.

A dead fly, on the other hand, did not inspire sympathy. She never thought it had died of starvation—flies
seemed capable of drawing nourishment from anything.

Instead she imagined it had died of stupidity, banging repeatedly into the glass pane of a window, or of old age, since they didn't live very long. Spiders could live for at least three years.

She wiped the top of the bookcase with a damp cloth and put the skull back down carefully, so as not to jar any more dirt onto the clean surface. She went through the house wiping down all the horizontal surfaces. She had to change the water in the basin seven times. Then she swept and mopped all the floors and vacuumed all the rugs. She cleaned some of the easier-to-reach windows, inside and out. This took several hours and she felt hungry and thirsty, so she got a glass of water and some buttered toast and surveyed her work. Although the place looked neater now and uncluttered, it still looked dirty. The stains were going to defeat her. New furniture, new carpets and fresh paint were needed, and at the moment they were beyond her means.

The bathroom and kitchen still had to be cleaned, but Margaret also wanted to work on the reconstruction today, so she decided to skip cleaning the stove and fridge altogether and do the bathroom and kitchen later. After all, it was only old friends who were coming over. They'd seen it all before. Would they really care if her house was clean? Besides, what made a good dinner party? Excellent food and company. You never heard someone say, "Oh I had a fabulous time at so-and-so's. Their house was *spotless!*" or conversely, "I had just the worst time at so-and-so's. What a pigsty!"

Working on the reconstruction had become increasingly important to Margaret since Monday's "attack of the furies." Tuesday she'd still been rattled, so she'd taken a couple of sleeping pills and dozed off and on or watched TV. But Wednesday she'd glued the whole skeleton in its permanent position. The work had been straightforward and mindless and soothing. Yesterday she'd modelled the cartilege of the nasal septum in slow-drying epoxy putty.

The work provided her a safe refuge, lulling her into a calm, peaceful kind of trance with sensual pleasures—the pleasures of shape and form and contour, the complex balance and structure of the skeleton, the air between the bones, the suppleness of modelling clay and the smell of it, of plaster and glue. And the silence.

The epoxy nasal septum had hardened so she decided to attach it. Its shape and orientation within the nasal cavity were determined by the degree to which the nose projected from the face. Normally, the clues for this were to be found in the nasal bones and the V-shaped depression that was the equivalent of the nasal spine at the bottom of the cavity, but these had not withstood weathering in Lucy. In his notes, Neill decided, based on other afarensis fossils, that the nose was probably still very apelike and projected, if at all, only minimally. She used slow-drying glue so she could fiddle with its position.

Then she rolled out some grey Plasticine to the thickness of the temporalis muscles. She determined the thickness by examining Neill's white plaster casts of that level of dissection in both chimpanzee and gorilla. She found the partially deconstructed grimacing plaster face casts interesting. They had come to feel familiar in her hands. She accepted their macabre wide grins the way she'd accepted the horrible parts of fairy tales as a child—they seemed familiar and natural.

She kneaded and shaped the muscle with her hands, then attached it to the skull. It converged into a tendon, which she joined to the coronoid process of the lower jaw. Using a fine sculpting tool, she then scored the side the way she'd noticed Neill had on the adult male. As she drew the lines with her scalpel it occurred to her that it was a strange thing to be doing. No one was ever going to see this level of the reconstruction, except for the few scientists who might want to examine photographs and casts, and those people would only care about measurements and proportions, not visual resemblance.

She began to wonder if Neill was a bit fanatical. He'd told her that one night when he was working late, he actually hallucinated the numbers of his measurements joining together and dancing wildly, rebelliously in a circle, then breaking loose and weaving off the page, laughing at his earnest obsessiveness. They refused to submit to him. The dancing escalated to a kind of bacchanalia and several numbers actually began to copulate and give birth to figures he'd never seen before.

She could see where the tension might arise to cause such a hallucination: he wanted each detail to be exact and right. This precision was impossible since the afarensis fossils did not yield nearly enough information. The fact that most decisions had to be, at best, informed guesses would have driven him crazy.

Frank had told her Neill lived a spartan existence, partly by choice. He was paid by the project, yet he devoted thousands of unpaid hours to his work. The museum tolerated repeated extensions of deadlines because the work he did was outstanding. Margaret thought if she were like Neill, she'd never complete anything. Like Avatar's frog, hopping each time half the distance to its goal and therefore never quite arriving, she'd get more and more obsessed by detail the closer she came to finishing a job.

She shaped the masseter muscles and attached them. First the deep portion of the muscles had to be attached at the zygomatic arch and down over the upper portion of the ramus. Then she attached the superficial portion—on the top to the zygomatic arch and on the bottom to the lower ramus.

She noticed as she concentrated on her work that she was wrinkling her nose and dilating her nostrils. She noticed it because the small muscles on the side of her nose felt strained holding this new expression. She also noticed that she was breathing entirely through her nostrils and they seemed completely free of mucus. With each breath they seemed to flare wider and the intake of air seemed less obstructed and more bountiful. She noticed that a brown apple core on her window sill smelled pleasantly like vanilla extract.

She took a photograph of the lower face from every angle and made a plaster cast.

That evening she opened her back door to the sound of dozens of wings beating as birds left the bird-feeder and relocated on the branches of the nearby fir. She needed to consider what she should do about John's birthday, which was marked beside today's date on her kitchen calendar. Until two months ago, John had been the most central person in her life. It didn't feel quite right to let the day pass without some kind of acknowledgment from her, yet she couldn't imagine a conversation without irony and awkwardness. Should she phone and wish him a happy birthday? It would be the first time they'd spoken in the seven weeks since he left. It occurred to her that *should* was not the right word any more. There was no should, no right way, no certainty, no protocol, no ritual.

That was one of the liberations of divorce. *Should*: the impersonal, the distancer, the anti-intimate. The cowardly. Now she would be forced to discover what she *wanted* to do, to flush out a true naked desire, an emotional commitment. "I'm doing this because I want to."

Did she want to phone John and wish him happy birthday...or not?

I don't *not* want to, she thought.

The bird-feeder was almost empty. Early evening sunlight illuminated the small backyard with a peachy glow and the smell of white apple blossoms filled the air. She was chilled briefly by the apple tree's shadow as she filled the feeder with seeds. She sprinkled some on the grass for the juncos, who were ground-feeders, and returned to the warmth of her back steps.

Chickadees flitted nervously back and forth between the branches of the fir and the branches of the apple, gradually moving closer to the feeder until one bold individual actually landed, snatched a seed in its beak and escaped to a higher-up branch, where it could hold the seed between long scaly toes and eat in peace.

Their name was a perfect onomatapoeia.

Chick-a-dee-dee-dee. "Chick-a-dee-dee-dee," her mother had sung one summer afternoon at Margaret's maternal grandmother's cottage. How young her mother had been—thirty-one—younger than Margaret now. She'd been relaxed that day, a respite from her usual depression, and during that small window she'd thought to imitate the bird for her daughter. Margaret wondered now if her mother's own mother had sung "Chick-a-dee-dee-dee" to her. Would her mother have been remembering that?

At the moment it seemed unlikely Margaret would have a child of her own, and she doubted she would ever sing the chickadee's call to her daughter or son. That moment would be isolated in her memory, the continuity broken, no sound fossil or memory fossil to leave a trace.

The chickadees were still tentative in their approach to the feeder. And for good reason. John had attached the bird-feeder to a rather low branch in the apple tree and it hung barely three feet from the ground. Their friend June had remarked once that what they had wasn't a bird-feeder at all, but a *cat*-feeder.

The birds cocked their heads first to one side, then to the other, as though they were asking the same question over and over. Then suddenly they flew in and snatched up a seed. She was glad of their caution. Often when she glanced out the kitchen window she'd notice a cat pressed flat to the ground, tail waving slowly from side to side, and she'd rap sharply on the windowpane to warn the birds and break the cat's concentration.

Every time she did this she thought how hypocritical her action was since she ate meat, meat from animals with more consciousness than birds, so why shouldn't cats? But her actions were instinctive, she seemed neurologically wired to warn and save other prey from predators.

She glanced into her neighbour's yard on the right. There was a small fir tree with a skirt of branches low to the ground under which the cats liked to hide. At the moment a white tail was twitching at the shadow's edge, a small white face with blue eyes peering out. Her window-rapping never had any effect on this cat because it was deaf.

Margaret felt a sudden quickness in the movement of her eyes, as though another set of eyes were darting glances through her own. Her interest in the cat changed. She watched closely, without moving. She checked and re-checked the cat's size—against the tree, the grass, the distance, making sure it was as small as it seemed. She didn't move a muscle, other than wrinkling her nose in concentration; she was waiting for the cat to catch a bird. Then she would startle it into dropping its kill. Saliva squirted into her mouth in anticipation.

It became difficult to stay still and she began feeling quite agitated. Slowly she reached down to a scab on her ankle and picked it and this eased her tension, despite the small pain as she neared the scab's centre. In fact, the pain was partly what eased the tension. Then the cat blinked, stood up and trotted toward the alley.

Margaret went back inside. The coolness of the house caused goosebumps to rise on her thighs and the backs of her arms. In the studio she picked up the gorilla skull from her worktable and sat down. She dialled John's number at work and transferred the receiver to the crook of her neck so she could examine the skull with both hands.

"Hi John, it's me. I'm phoning to wish you happy birthday," she said, a slight challenge and a slight apology in her tone.

"Oh…thanks," he said guardedly. He was wondering if wishing him happy birthday was merely a pretext; he was wondering what her real agenda was. She could hear suspicion in the pauses between his words.

"How are you?" she asked gently, not knowing what else to say and hoping a caring tone might ease his wariness.

"I'm fine, Margaret," he said in a patiently forbearing tone. He seemed to have decided not to ask how she was. His silence posed the question—what do you want?

She shouldn't have called.

The porous, thinner bone around the nasal aperture of the skull was shell-like. Its grey-white colour was like the outside of an oyster shell, the colour of calcium. Bone seemed inanimate compared to flesh, an involuntary structure of the body. How amazing that something like this could be created from simple elements—plants, water.

"How are you?" John asked at last, sighing, realizing she was not going to say anything until he did.

He didn't want to know how she was. She had become inanimate to him.

"Fine." Then she slipped into her familiar role of facilitator and began chatting away about the reconstruction. *What a ninny*, she thought as she heard herself laughing gaily. *You sound so false.*

"That's good," John commented with a smidgeon of goodwill.

"And my teeth are a disaster area it turns out. Right after you left"—the first time either of them had mentioned it—"I got a really bad toothache. Now I have an appointment every week for the entire summer, and you know how much I like going to the dentist."

She heard herself trying to restore at least the illusion

of familiarity between them. It was amazing that in such a short time she and John had gone from sharing a home, a life and a future to having no connection at all. What they shared was even more negative than no connection—they shared an intense disconnection. A wounding, dying subtext. There was less potential for intimacy than with a complete stranger.

The image of John's feet and calves came to mind; she'd always been fascinated by their maleness, by their difference from hers. They were so sinewy and hard and white. Whenever she stared at John's feet, the image of Christ's feet nailed to the cross flickered across her mind.

It was hard to believe she'd ever seen John's bare feet now. Harder still to believe she'd lain naked beside him, that they'd slept in the same bed for ten years, heard the idiosyncratic sounds of each other's digestive systems. Seen each other's ungroomed self.

"That's too bad. Are you still in pain?" Such careful words, solicitous, professional, distancing.

She didn't want him to think she'd phoned for sympathy. "No, it's no big deal really. It's just the needles. How's your work? Busy as ever?"

Yes, busy. He sounded weary, but not lonely, not unhappy. Entrenched. Guarding his separateness, his right to live outside her reality and the scope of her needs, free of his failure to meet them, or rather free of any guilt about his unwillingness to meet them.

Their separation did not seem to have called very much into question for him. It had not shaken the foundations of his identity. If anything it had confirmed who he was. He could relax now, and be himself.

Her eyes narrowed. Bastard. His equilibrium was

founded on indifference, smugness, a cowardly refusal to risk himself, she thought vindictively, smugly, pettily. His was a garrison soul, hoarding itself. Future lovers would have to "accept him for who he was," or he would cut them off swiftly and without regret.

There had been a long silence on the phone line.

"Thanks for calling." He did not successfully disguise his relief at nearing the end of the conversation. "I guess we'll be in touch."

"No rush," Margaret said, unable to hold back a note of bitterness. "I've got a lot on my plate right now."

Her memories sometimes seemed so random. Why did she remember what she did—not important moments, only small details, like John's fingers running through his hair when he read the newspaper, slowly, relishing each strand, or that, when he was about to make a point, he would lay his left index finger alongside his nose. She remembered where he tended to get pimples and the way his flesh hung, more puckered and loose when he was tired. She did not remember these details with any particular emotion, she remembered them as facts, a list.

"Okay. See you later," he said.

She looked down vaguely and was disconcerted to find the skull staring up at her from between her thighs, as though it might have just popped out in a bloodless labour.

She gazed around the studio and felt as though she had no physical presence in the room. She could touch nothing, effect nothing. It was as though her corporeal self were stuck in the immediate past, unable to get itself unsnagged.

She heard the dial tone and lowered the receiver

slowly onto the cradle.

Better to have loved and lost than never to have loved at all. No. *Better to have never lost at all.* Loss was bigger than love. A permanent external landscape, waiting to consume a person and transform her into a walking zombie.

Perhaps this was why she was unable to remember happy moments from her childhood. And why she didn't remember happy moments from her marriage. The moments were there—*some* moments, anyway.

Sunday afternoons when her father played opera records and her mother drank a glass of sweet sherry, the smell of a cooking roast wafting through the house. No one spoke much. She was old enough to read books without pictures. She had a favourite blanket, a Scottish mohair in reds and blues and purples that reflected a deep warmth back to the marrow of her bones. Safety, warmth, fullness, peace, accompaniment.

What was the point of remembering lost happiness? Nothing to be gained except a heightened awareness of loss. Of course every moment lived is immediately lost, she knew this. Life was loss, a hemorrhage of loss right from the beginning.

She closed her eyes and imagined a bone gleaming briefly at the bottom of a hole, then disappearing deeper into the earth, like a splinter—the more she tried to dig it out, the deeper it got buried in her flesh. She napped.

When she woke it was from some other dream. *Flesh into dust.*

Flesh walking through dust, watching, listening. Walking through a world of ash. Was there a child?

Pad, pad, pad. Like a snowfall, the pure quiet, every sound distinctive and separate as a stone. She hesitated, turned, looked back at her child who was gazing around in quiet wonder. Infinity temporarily collapsed into the moment, their past and future stretched out around them like a warm blanket. The ash puffed up with each step and coated the hair on the back of her calves. She looked back again at her child and for a moment felt no more protective of its small body than of her own. Protectiveness seemed irrelevant in this wonderland of soft quiet death.

Out of the corner of her eye she sees the bird flitting from tree to tree, her child holding out an arm, pointing to it. Margaret had always thought of infinity and death as darkness, as a black universe with little pins of light, not as this soft light-grey world.

SEVENTEEN

"Lettuce, radish, onions, garlic, whipping cream, coffee, strawberries, tomatoes, parsley, dust-mop, toilet paper, finish jaw, reread Ecclesiastes, think about the word appetite."

Her brain worked in lists. Every day had a list that ticked away in the background. From her waitress days, she thought.

In the supermarket's vegetable section the produce had just been sprayed and it glistened. The word "roughage" came to mind—green things tickling their way through the bowels, getting into those soft crevices and wrinkles and gently brushing away all the foul garbage—roughage, ruffles, purple kale, radish tops and lettuce. Verdant lace collars. A good scrub for the innards. Restoring the vital flow.

She wondered about the state of her own innards as

she pushed the cart to the dairy section. How unclean were they? How stagnant? How teeming with bacteria? She recalled photographs of healthy lungs she'd seen in anti-smoking pamphlets. Nothing could be *that* clean and pink and elastic in her body. They must have been taken from someone very young. Living organisms degenerate quickly. While memory flourishes.

She immersed the tomatoes briefly in scalding water, then peeled and seeded them. The translucent orangey-red skins and the fleshy red pulp were succulently beautiful. She sliced the fruit in halves, quarters, opening fertile chambers of glistening seed clusters coated in slippery clear membrane. It was pleasurable inserting her thumb and squirting the seeds into the mulch bucket, satisfying to know they would lend their fecundity to her garden.

Another evocative word, mulch. Connoting rich, dark earth, filled with nutrients, moist, fertile, waiting for the roots of flowers and vegetables to gorge on its abundance.

The house was as she'd left it when she stopped cleaning yesterday, except that she'd wiped the bathroom counter and cleaned the toilet this morning. She'd worked on the jaw the rest of yesterday and all day today in between shopping and cooking. Adding even a small area of flesh profoundly changed the way the reconstruction looked. It wasn't a skeleton any more, it was more alive and more compelling. It was becoming something.

The doorbell rang. David and June stood on the front porch, David holding a bunch of freesias and irises and

June holding a bottle of wine. They had dressed up a little. David wore a black jacket over a red T-shirt and jeans and June wore a richly printed paisley cotton tunic over black tights. Helen's old Volvo pulled up behind their second-hand Audi and she honked and swung open her car door. She wore her usual jeans and T-shirt, but also lipstick and earrings, and Margaret liked this casual concession to dressing up. Margaret suddenly felt how much she'd cut herself off from her friends since John had left.

The sun was setting and pink light filled the living room. The three friends took off their jackets and put down bags amid greetings of welcome and questions about each other's lives. Margaret ushered them through to the kitchen, put the flowers in a vase and offered drinks. She handed David the corkscrew and bottle of wine.

Helen went over to the stove and lifted the lid from a pot to see what was for dinner.

"Ew!"

Small islands of green mould floated in the remnants of red spaghetti sauce.

"Put that lid back on and don't be so nosy." Margaret had made a cold summer pasta sauce to be served on hot spaghetti. It was in the fridge.

Margaret felt buoyed by her friends' presence. It drove the chill and emptiness of her house away.

"Where's John?" David asked, looking around the kitchen as though John's name might cause him to appear.

Margaret doubted her friends would miss John. Everyone had been pleasant enough and friendly and made an effort, but it always remained that—an effort.

Even their most successful evenings as a group lacked a really natural flow. When Margaret told them about the separation no one looked completely surprised or particularly unhappy. Helen asked when he'd left and scolded Margaret for not confiding in them earlier.

"It's quite an odd feeling, eating dinner with all these bones about," David said eventually, ducking his head toward his plate to get a forkful of spaghetti into his mouth before it unravelled.

Wisps of diaphanous green material from the hummingbird's wings floated about their feet. Margaret hadn't swept under the table, thinking she should wait until the last minute because she would still be working on the reconstruction. Then she'd forgotten about it.

Her worktable had been transformed into an attractive dining table with a huge vase of purple and white lilacs, colourful Indian hand-dyed placemats, her grandmother's silver and her mother's crystal. She'd moved the three skulls to the top of the filing cabinet where they sat facing the dinner guests. Behind them the stuffed hummingbird was poised to take flight. On low shelving under the window Neill's dissection casts were lined up with their agonizing grimaces. The walls were covered with sketches of Lucy, photocopies of Neill's drawings of the male afarensis and photographs of apes, including humans. In one corner file folders, books and miscellaneous papers were stacked against the wall. In front of these stood the reconstruction, like a severely worm-eaten sentinel. It too faced the dining table.

The guests' cheeks gleamed and their eyes shone in the candlelight while around them loomed skulls, bones and pithecoid forms lit by dim flickers of light and shadow from the small flames on the dining table.

"It's a bit lugubrious," June said. "Are you sure you're all right?"

"Yes, I'm fine. Just fine. It's a good time for introspection," Margaret answered, "and bones lend themselves well to introspection."

Now that her separation was out in the open she was under scrutiny, every nuance examined for signs of her emotional state, their sympathy implicit in every remark and gesture. This was exactly what she had wanted to avoid. She needed to recreate herself slowly, cleanly, privately. She wanted to reshape herself in the emotionally hygienic solitude of her cocoon.

Entertaining felt as though someone had torn open the chrysalis and exposed the dreaming pupa inside. It was as though her face itself had been a mask and it had been torn off, leaving a blank, indeterminate gash with eyes, nose, mouth and ears intact. Her friends tried not to stare, but they couldn't quite look at her normally.

Margaret had first become friends with David at art school. When they graduated, David was hired as a graphic artist by a large advertising agency, but he quickly became disenchanted. He went back to school to study film and decided to specialize in editing because he could work alone in a controlled environment. He loved the detail and precision of his work. He'd also begun to grow bonsais and he liked to carve small figurines in rosewood. He and June met while he was working in advertising. She dropped out of the business the year after him and she was drifting now, dissatisfied with her job, which was some administrative government position.

When David found out what Margaret was working on he immediately wanted to see the replica fossils. She opened up the case where she had repacked them and took out the lower jaw. He held it up to the candlelight, turning its cluster of dark teeth this way and that in the unstable light.

"Ugh. Put that thing away. You don't know where it's been or what exotic strains of disease it might be carrying." June grimaced and moved her plate away.

David pushed his plate aside and laid the jawbone on the table.

"No really, David. It's too much. Put it back in the box until we're finished dinner," June insisted, coming back from the kitchen with a cloth to wipe the table where the bone had been.

"It's not a real bone, June. It's just a very good cast," Margaret said. "But they can find out amazing things from real fossil teeth. What an individual ate, and by extension what kind of climate and landscape they lived in. If you study the wear patterns under a microscope you can find out more or less what an individual ate for breakfast, lunch and dinner millions of years ago."

One tooth could reveal so much of the distant past, yet the recent past could be buried and concealed in the brain forever, Margaret thought as she remembered—amazed she had forgotten—that she'd had sex with David. It seemed to her it should be a dream.

"What an awful idea," June said. "No privacy, even across millions of years. Some *person* I don't even know might dig up my teeth and discover what I ate during my lifetime. I don't tell anyone that. Not even David."

"Ah, but can they tell how *much* you ate? That could be the embarrassing part," Helen said.

"You can tell if someone starved or suffered from malnutrition. I don't know if you can tell whether they were fat."

"Well I suppose a skeleton by definition doesn't have a weight problem," Helen said. "The severest form of anorexia. Clothes finally hang elegantly. One small compensation for being dead—at last you can eat anything and not gain weight."

It had been during their first year at art school, before John and before June. They'd both been lonely and had liked each other immediately. They saw films like Hitchcock's *Vertigo* and discussed narcissism, the act of transforming the world into mirrors of the self and Hitchcock's mirror symbols—lakes, rear-view mirrors, the abyss, the eyes of another person. They discussed the essential sado-masochistic structure of every intimate relationship. Together they imagined having power and, laughing with relish, how it might corrupt them. In all their joyfully intense conversations they felt they intuited the subtext and nuance and irony implicit in each other's pronouncements.

Once he'd touched her hand among the plates and glasses and salt and pepper shakers on the cafeteria table. Though they had not acted that day, it was understood they were going to have sex.

It only happened a couple of times. David was not someone who lived in his body. He scorned men in locker rooms, sweating together, and he did not seek out physical exertion. He was a man dedicated to the life of the mind and his body reflected his dedication. His flesh was soft and the bones could be felt easily underneath.

She looked at David's mouth now as he spoke and cringed as she remembered kissing it. She never liked thinking about sexual acts with former lovers. It occurred to her that she might be a serial monogamist. But Phillip? Certainly in deed she hadn't been monogamous. Yet perhaps she had been monogamous in thought because after she made love with Phillip she'd kind of vacated herself from John. When she made love with him again after Philip she'd almost felt nauseated by the confusion of bodies. After nine years of marriage John had been made unfamiliar to her in one night. When she went to touch his slender wiry body, which she knew so well, the image of Phillip's body flickered across her mind, and she became disoriented in a confusing geography of male bodies. How did she usually touch John, how did she caress him? She couldn't remember.

Eventually she'd re-entered a shell of intimacy with John, but the last threads of attachment to him had been broken. She stopped looking to him, however despairingly, for sex or love.

"Margaret, you've hardly touched your dinner. I'm ready for seconds and I don't want to look like a pig," Helen said.

"I always lose my appetite when I'm the hostess. You know what it's like with your own cooking. Your taste-buds get saturated or something from smelling it cook."

The phone rang and Margaret left the table to answer it. It was Neill. He assumed she was free to talk and launched into telling her that he wanted to change the display's story.

"I've decided the male is too passive. Lucy has her moment of hesitation, which is quite powerful, but there's no story for the male."

"Neill, I'm right in the middle of dinner and I have guests."

"Oh. Well I just wanted to tell you I've called a meeting next Friday at 1:30 to discuss this. Can you be there?"

"I guess so. Wouldn't it be better if I just kept working? You don't really need me, do you?" Margaret did not want to leave her house.

"You can't make it?"

"I can."

"You should come. It's possible we'll have to do separate storyboards for the male and the female. I want something more dramatic for the male. I want to emphasize how muscular and powerful he was. Perhaps confronting a baboon or another male. They were even stronger than chimpanzees, and physical strength would have been a survival characteristic back then."

Margaret doubted physical strength would have been much of a factor against the jaws of big cats like leopards or the powerful coil of a python. Her emerging conception of afarensis was of a predominantly anxious creature. When could they relax? Perhaps while mating and perhaps when they were infants and their mothers were responsible for their survival. There were so many hazards: hunger, drought, falling into a river, floods, parasites, viruses, bacteria and most of all the anxiety of still being part of the food chain—lions, leopards, snakes.

After a pause Margaret said, "Perhaps they were quite shy. People might identify with that. The fact that they didn't have fire or houses or fences or electricity or weapons. Just their own bodies in a world full of predators, disease and hunger."

"When parents are glazing over after an afternoon of buying ice cream and saying yes and no to their kids, who are overstimulated and running from one thing to the next, you have to come up with something compelling, something that will strike people's emotional chords, like terror, love, victory, death."

"The smaller moments can be interesting too."

Neill was starting to disagree when Margaret heard June's voice rising in irritation from the dining room and she remembered she'd abandoned her guests in the middle of dinner. She excused herself firmly. Neill offered her a lift to the meeting on Friday and she accepted and said goodbye.

When she came back Helen was talking and David and June were eating their spaghetti with stony expressions. Margaret guessed their bickering had flared slightly past the usual limits and she felt anxious, as though her job as hostess was to smooth things over, create a diversion, steer the evening back to agreeable and pleasant territory.

"Where were we? Oh yes, teeth. Did you know there are microscopic ripples on the top of the incisor which are separated by lines? Each line represents about seven days' growth, so if the fossil is infant or juvenile you can discover the age quite precisely by counting the lines. It's amazing. And the wonderful thing is, teeth last the longest of all the body parts, so there are a relative plenitude of them in the fossil record."

Helen laughed. "That's the opposite of when you're

alive. Then they're the first to go. Even children get cavities. Don't you think it's incredible that we need a whole separate doctor just for teeth, and you have to see him twice as often as the physician who takes care of the entire rest of your body?"

Margaret smiled absently at Helen. She was having trouble making the transition from talking to Neill about Lucy to this social group, with its more complex currents. She couldn't think of anything else to say and there was an extended moment of silence.

"I was telling David and June," Helen eventually said, "that the discovery of evolution, and more particularly the evolution of Homo sapiens from a shared ancestry with apes, shattered people's sense of themselves in the West more profoundly than Copernicus. They suffered from pithecophobia, a profound aversion to apes, and beasts in general. It was too much to expect people to make the adjustment from seeing themselves as the crowning glory of creation to seeing themselves as the random result of lucky—for them—mutations."

Helen was working on a Master's degree in the History of Science Department and her thesis was on how the ethical and social standards of Victorian England and the burgeoning scientific knowledge of the time influenced each other. She was concentrating particularly on deconstructing contemporary assumptions about "race" that lingered from the Victorian paradigm.

"Ape is nothing," David said. "We go back to a kind of marsupial to a shrew to fish to probably some relative of the amoeba." He spoke toward his plate, not to anyone in particular and with no apparent expectation of being heard.

When everyone had finished their second helpings Margaret went into the kitchen to put the kettle on and whip some cream for strawberry shortcake. She poured the liquid into a large measuring cup, then wiped the thick paste that collected round the bottle's rim onto her finger and scraped it off on the cup's edge. The noise of the electric beaters isolated her totally from her guests and she relaxed.

Part of Neill's research notes relating to the reconstruction of the jaw addressed facial expressions. He surmised Lucy would have had some expressions in common with chimpanzees and gorillas—frowning, open-mouthed play face, threatening sneer and open- and closed-mouthed fear grins. She'd looked up photographs of these expressions in her reference books. As the beaters made wide ripples and folds in the cream she found her face exploring a chimpanzee sneer. The expression, though not one she'd had cause to use in her adult life, felt natural on her mouth. She needed longer lips and a more forward-thrusting mouth to do it properly, of course, but she thought she was close.

Helen came in with the rest of the dinner dishes. Margaret's back was to her so she had time to rearrange her face before her friend came into view. She finished whipping the cream and dispatched Helen back to the dining room licking one beater and carrying the other for David or June. She sipped from her fourth glass of wine. The alcohol was beginning to make her feel as though things were happening too quickly and she felt a little wild and out of control. She poured sliced sugared strawberries over the bottom half of the shortcake, dolloped on a thick layer of cream, placed the top half of the shortcake on, more whipped cream, and tumbled the rest of the strawberries over the peak. She'd practise the sneer later in front of the mirror. She presented the shortcake in all its bulging red and white opulence to her friends in the dining room.

Helen was talking again: "...human foundling, nurtured and brought up by a group of apes, happy and at one with nature except for an occasional nameless yearning. Tarzan meets a human female, falls in love and follows her to decadent civilization like a lamb to the slaughter."

"Like Adam and Eve and Pandora's Box," said David with phony cheerfulness. "Women are always ruining a guy's fun, seducing him from his oneness with the world and bringing on the evils of civilization."

"I loved the scene where Tarzan," Helen continued, "or Graystoke rather, that beautiful French actor, what was his name, Christian something, makes love with Jane for the first time and he gets so excited he goes ape and starts jumping up and down on the bed and hooting."

"Tarzan doesn't even meet Jane until he gets to England," June said acidly. "So his fall happens well before he even meets her. In fact, she's the only redemptive figure."

Helen looked at Margaret and rolled her eyes in exasperation. She persevered. "Lots of Gothic tales began to arise of monstrous offspring from unnatural unions between beautiful women and beasts. The circumstances of conception were always left modestly vague."

"I don't think there's much history of bestiality where women are concerned," June said restlessly.

"The stories centre on the terrible shame of the birth.

The woman would keep her baby locked away in the cellar and years later the poor creature would finally die from lack of love."

"A common enough destiny," David added, glancing at June.

"Look you two, cut it out," Helen said. "These stories were not about the war between the sexes. They were about human consciousness being trapped in the body of an animal. They were about people trying to come to terms with the brute side of their history, and with the loss of their anthropomorphic universe. The soul inside the beast would try to communicate itself to its beautiful young mother, but all she could see was a hairy hand reaching out to her from the darkness, a symbol of her shame and her unacceptable self."

"Women are just so *unperceptive*," David went on. "They always fail to see the noble intelligence behind our brute physicality."

"On the contrary," said June. "We usually fail to see the brute lurking so close to the surface behind the human being."

Margaret had closed her eyes and was drifting on alcoholic waves of thought. From behind her eyelids everything suddenly got dark and she wondered if she was blacking out, and then she thought four glasses of wine couldn't be enough for that, so she opened her eyes. The candles were still flickering but all the other lights were out.

"Must be a power outage," David said.

"Let's blow out the candles. This is a great chance to experience pure darkness," Helen said. "Where are the matches first? Okay."

The moon was half full, and gradually they were able to make out through the window the shadowy branches of the fir tree, the unmowed lawn in the backyard and the silhouette of one another's heads and shoulders.

"Can you serve the cake in the dark?" David asked.

"Sure. There's enough light from the moon." Margaret gently pressed the knife on the shortcake and sawed. Everyone was quiet while the cake was served, then there was the light *ting* as dessert forks made contact with china.

"I can feel those skulls staring at me," June said.

"Mmmm," said Helen, appreciating the shortcake.

The whole neighbourhood was suspended, peaceful. Margaret imagined hands reaching out in the dark searching for candles, matches, and people thinking this is what it was like in the old days, before electricity. The children who were still awake saw their houses in candlelight. They marvelled at the leaping shadows as they were led to bed by candlelight and begged to be allowed to keep a candle in their room to go to sleep by. The limbs of lovers glowed as they discovered new images of themselves and each other in the soft wavering orange light. Even the folds of the bedding looked voluptuous.

Margaret felt very light and free, as though gravity were merely a trampoline, a force that allowed her to push off and jump higher. The feeling reminded her of a night on a high school field trip. She and a boy she liked had snuck out of the dorms and met outside in the snow. It would have been the year before her mother died. He'd put a pair of jeans on over his pyjamas and boots and she was wearing just a long white flannel nightgown and her boots. The boy had brought a white sweater and he gave it to her chivalrously to put on. They began walking over the moonlit snow. She discovered that because she was wearing all white she dissolved into the whiteness around her and the effect was of floating over the snow, as though she were an angel and there were only snow or air between her eyes and her boots. She'd been able to stride out effortlessly, while her friend in his dark clothes struggled behind her through the snow.

She felt free like that again. And unusually clear-headed. She started telling a story in the darkness. The voice was just suddenly there inside her, unselfconscious, ready to speak.

"Once upon a time there were two people, a boy and a girl, chained in a dungeon. Their cells were side by side but both imagined the other was living upstairs with their beautiful young mother whom they heard moving softly from room to room, her flowing gown whispering against itself, her voice hushed and gentle. Each felt abandoned, ugly and grief-stricken, chained to the black walls of their lightless dungeon, while they imagined the other upstairs in a world of light.

"They sat, day in and day out, filthy, inarticulate and forlorn and heard the faint clanking of other chains, and slowly they began to understand that someone else was also locked away in the basement of the house.

"After that they often stood, hands pressed against the cold black wall, listening in silence, yearning for an impression, or warmth, a sound from the other prisoner, some proof there was someone else there with them. Sometimes they imagined someone just like themselves, and sometimes they imagined a monster, or a beautiful sad angel whose feathery wings trailed in the filth. They sang poignant melodies to the other being through the wall, but only the sound of chains was ever heard on the other side.

"Over the years white handprints began to appear on either side of the black wall, formed by the burning intensity of their yearning. These ghostly white handprints and the sound of chains were the only evidence they ever got that they were not alone."

She opened her eyes again. Someone had relit the candles and she saw her friends' faces in the warm glow. Yearning and the sound of chains. The impression that a life of beauty and radiance was going on elsewhere, upstairs, in a world you're shut out of. All the while it's there in the fevered pressing against a black wall, in the miracle of a handprint and the singing of angels reverberating off stone, sounding like chains.

EIGHTEEN

That night she dreamed of a starved dog curled up
on rags beginning to gnaw on its own leg.

He snarled at her when she tried to approach, thinking she was trying to steal his leg from him, his dinner. As he continued to gnaw at his flesh she saw some white bone showing through the gristle and tendons and pink flesh.

She was both the person trying to approach the dog and she was also the dog. It was only the person who experienced pain. She winced and writhed at the sight of the dog's teeth sinking into its own flesh. The dog was so far gone he didn't know what he was doing.

Then she was on a living-room couch, kissing John. They were teenagers. She was trying to suppress an urge to bite him. She was afraid she would bite his lips off.

She didn't want him to know he was in danger,

because then he would stop kissing her, but the urge was becoming irrepressible, the biting reflex twitching in the muscles of her jaw. She drew back in horror and ran out of the room, her jaw snapping uncontrollably the way a cat's does watching birds through a window.

NINETEEN

She went downstairs next morning in an old Led Zeppelin T-shirt and her underwear. The T-shirt was ripped at the arm and the neck hole was stretched and droopy. It dated back to a concert she'd gone to when she was sixteen or seventeen with her second boyfriend. She'd had a great time, her first Dionysian experience. She'd surrendered herself completely to the music and the crowd. Afterwards he'd bought the T-shirt for her. She couldn't believe it was sixteen years old now.

She put the kettle on and went into her studio. The table was strewn with the remains of dinner: dessert plates smeared with whipped cream stained bright pink with strawberry juice; crystal goblets, some still half filled with red wine, marked with greasy fingerprints and semicircles of lipstick. In the midst of all the remains was Lucy's lower jaw. An empty jaw surrounded by empty plates, as though, under cover of dark, the jaw had swallowed all the food. It seemed vaguely threatening to her. She started stacking plates on the side farthest away from the jaw.

When the power came back on, just before everyone left, David had asked if Margaret had a human jaw he could look at. It too lay on the table beside the irises and freesias. Compared to Lucy's it looked so ingrown, overcrowded and over-refined. Decadent. She imagined the two jaws, australopithecine and human, singing a song of triumph and feasting. A slick song, gloating over the deaths of others. There was something ironic about a carnivore mouth singing. All that decaying scavenged flesh, the lifeblood of others. Sing, sing! All that swallowed last-minute pain, digested consciousness.

She finished cleaning the table off and moved the reconstruction back out of the corner. She felt somehow uneasy about the night before—a residue of irritation that increased her desire to work, to speak to no one, to protect herself from socializing. She felt too raw, too vulnerable, as though she'd said the wrong things and exposed parts of herself she wouldn't have consciously chosen to expose.

Over the next few days she formed and attached the obicularis oris, levator labii superioris complex, levator angular oris and the two depressor muscles of the mouth. Then she formed the risorius muscle and attached it to fascia over the masseter muscle, drew it across the cheek and attached it to the corners of the mouth.

On Wednesday she formed the nasal muscles that attached to the upper jawbone under the upper border of the orbicularis oris and went up, over and beside the nose. Then she brought together the fibres of various other maxillary muscles to form the nodes at the corner of the mouth.

The lips were slightly parted and the tips of the reconstruction's teeth showed. Margaret felt the heat of its breath passing out between them, leaving a thin film of moisture on the lips that quickly evaporated in the heat. The breath smelled of fruit being broken down, fermented and rotting molecules, the stink of living made warm and moist in the lungs. She breathed in. Hot dusty air carried the taste of ash into her mouth.

Under the smell of ash lay the smell of the savanna, a warm rich grassy smell, the smell of earth never frozen. She could distinguish the scent of different faeces melting back into the earth, the large piles left by giraffes, the smaller tubes of gazelle, the pellets of rodents. The air carried a faint whiff of sweet mountain air, and the occasional waft of coolness from a river.

She thought of the smell of snow. Like cold air that lay on the surface of a glacial river or mountain lake. The smell of the season's first snowfall. A smell Lucy never knew. The smell of everything else going dormant, covered over by the clear smell of coldness.

The world became one colour and one texture. She remembered the silence. The background roar of car engines suddenly absent, except for the occasional whine of spinning tires and the last few buses driven by the gamer bus drivers. Her father called her on the telephone. Come home. It was the other side of town. I don't think I can get there in this weather. He said he had something important to tell her. Tell me over the phone. I think it would be better if you were here when

I told you. I can't get there in this weather. What's so important all of a sudden? Your mother's dead.

A brain hemorrhage. She walked to her parents' home through the snow. It took four hours. Imagining her mother's brain inside its dark skull, drowning in blood, pushed in on all sides by blood that had nowhere else to go. Had it leaked out of her ears? It seemed odd to be thinking about blood in all that white snow.

Night fell when she was about halfway there. Streetlamps revealed myriad flakes in their skirts of light plummeting down to earth. She walked purposefully. She just wanted to be beside her mother, to wrap a warm blanket around her and cradle and comfort her. Her father had told her that the ambulance had removed the body but somehow she hadn't connected that that would mean her mother's body would no longer be there in her house.

She tried to summon her mother's face alive, with blood, so she could freeze it in her memory, but her mind jumped around and the face kept dissolving behind snowflakes, smiling wistfully, already a construction of Margaret's mind and not the woman herself. How could a face disappear so quickly from memory? Perhaps you never really remember faces as much as recognize them. But you don't realize this because you don't really need to until someone dies.

Although she couldn't fix her mother's face in her mind, she did remember her voice. Trudging through the silent, blanketed world, past the windows of houses filled with warm yellow light, she heard her mother's clear low voice echo the song of the chickadee.

She added the fibro-fatty tissue and lesser nasal cartileges to the reconstruction's nose until all it needed was skin. It was very broad and flat.

"Hello?"

"Hi, it's Helen. I've been phoning you since Sunday. I wanted to thank you for Saturday night. It was a good evening. Listen, that story you told in the dark—the kids in the dungeon. What was that all about? It was so vivid. And, if you don't mind my saying, very personal."

"It's the first time I've ever done anything like that. I don't really know what it meant."

"Well, now that you ask, you seemed odd... We all like our privacy, Margaret, but I must say it bugged me that you didn't even tell me you'd split with John."

"I know. I'm sorry. But it's sort of embarrassing somehow. I feel like a failure. And I don't really want to talk about it yet. You get so symbiotic in a marriage. I don't really know who I am any more."

"But it's not healthy to cut yourself off totally. You need to have some fun. Come out and play. Let's go see a movie."

"Helen, I'm too scared sometimes to even get out of bed. I'm paralysed except in my work right now, so I'm just going to stick to that."

"What're you afraid of?"

"Well, death."

"Well, who isn't?"

"Not death exactly. It's more like because I know I'm going to die, when I really let myself believe it, every moment becomes irrevocable and pointless at the same time. It makes it hard to even breathe."

"Margaret, that's a bit abstract, don't you think? I mean aren't you supposed to deal with that kind of existential stuff when you're a teenager?"

She looked at the shadow between the lips, between the teeth. How could a whole body vanish into that small hole, down that small passageway? It seemed miraculous that creatures could disappear forever into another animal's mouth.

"Helen, I've got to go. I can't let the clay dry. Thanks so much for calling... I'll talk to you."

The pupil was quite dilated. The iris was a deep brown with lighter flecks and the rest of the eyeball was a bluey white navigated by tiny capillaries. It yellowed in the middle and was redder toward the back. Neill had made the eyeballs but wouldn't tell her how, which irritated her. What did he think? She was going to try and sell his method to the competition? What competition? The wax museum?

The slow-drying modelling clay allowed her to adjust the orientation of the eyeballs in the skull until the gaze converged at about twenty-five feet. Margaret was working toward an expression consistent with Lucy looking at a bird alighting on an ash-covered branch. When the fine muscles around the eye and skin were added, the gaze would be both dreamy and startled, curious, a bit awestruck.

"Facial expressions shouldn't be too extreme," Neill had written in his notes. "If an expression is too violent or excessive in any way, it makes comparisons with other species much more difficult."

Without the surrounding soft tissue the effect of the

naked eyeballs was quite startling. The reconstruction looked by turns either terrified or astonished. And Margaret was suddenly aware of its gaze on her constantly. Its peripheral vision, unblinkered by flesh, seemed to cover almost 360 degrees, so even when she stood beside it she felt it looking at her out of the corner of its eye.

Even when she went to the bathroom she was aware of the creature staring between her shoulder blades as she retreated, and then alone in the studio, gazing nakedly into space.

She formed the orbicularis oculi, a large sphincter muscle that circumscribed both the orbit and the eyelid. Then she stood back and looked at the head. The eyes, nose and mouth were reconstructed to the level just before skin, yet she had trouble visualizing what the final face would look like.

She wished she could sculpt the reconstruction. She wanted to create Lucy texturally, expressively, artistically. She was frustrated with the slow, plodding work of anatomical reconstruction, its lack of fluidity, its dead precision. With working blindly from the inside out.

For a moment she considered phoning Neill and suggesting that she sculpt the hands, feet, legs and trunk instead. Once the fur was on, no one would be able to tell the difference anyway. And it would save a lot of time.

But she knew his answer already. Besides, she realized it wasn't a realistic version of Lucy she wanted to sculpt. What she wanted was to sculpt a face that in some way showed a human female and Lucy like palimpsests of each other. She wanted to sculpt a human female and make her face melt into Lucy's features, to reveal concretely, explicitly, the genetic echo Margaret was beginning to feel in her own cells, in her own muscles, in the small movements of her own face. She wanted to create a figure with volume and mass that would explore how intimately, physically connected she was to this primitive ancestor, in every muscle, ligament and bone. She wanted to get a piece of stone under her hands again and begin excavating these images, begin chipping and chiselling them out.

The right pressure.

Who is in there?

Tap, tap, tap.

The right tool. *Tap, tap.* At the right angle.

On some level she knows who, but consciously it's still a mystery to her. A face. A heavily ridged brow, sockets deep, burning. An anguished, passionate, self-contained wounding. The cave of the eyes. Dark, quick. Two embers, glowing and alive in darkness.

Bone.

Soft organic stone, giving structure to flesh. As rock gives topographical contour to the earth. This face is like an old mountain, worn down and rounded by erosion. Buried and unknown. You chisel away at the face of stone and reveal another complete face inside. Perhaps with the right tools you can reach the first particle of being.

Tap, tap.

Who is in there?

Neill came by the house to see her reconstruction and to pick her up for the committee meeting he'd called that

Friday. He had a quibble about the nose; he wanted it even flatter than she'd built it, the nostrils even less distinct, more like holes. She'd been expecting more criticism, so she was quite pleased.

At the beginning of the meeting Frank made his usual small speech. "Do we want to emphasize the primitiveness of Australopithecus afarensis or the primitiveness of Homo sapiens? Museums are about connections and we want our visitors to connect themselves with the creatures in the display. We want them to think about evolution as more than abstract scientific theory. We want them to think of it as their personal history—the history of their own emotions and all their perceptions of the universe. The history of their bodies. We want our visitors to come away aware of themselves as part of one branch in the great ape family."

Neill spoke next. "Obviously the Laetoli footprints are powerful, but as it stands the display is too static. Lucy is off in a world of her own—*hesitating*—and perhaps that is interesting and dynamic in itself but it leaves the male just *standing*. There's no expression to give the male in this context. He's just standing there."

The museum staff writer, Matthew, suggested creating a subtext for the display, a backstory. "There are some interesting parallels between the Adam and Eve story and evolution. The two in the display, the male and female, do symbolically represent the beginning of the human species.

"Lucy might be a lower-ranking female frustrated in her efforts to rise in the dominance hierarchy. A strange male approaches the band. She aggressively keeps other females in estrus away from him and goes off with him herself for a few days. Tension increases between Lucy and the other females and between the stranger and the other males until Lucy and the stranger are forced out of the group. Perhaps this occurs when food is scarce, and the two are chased right out of the band's territory."

At a certain point Margaret stopped hearing Matthew's words and just watched his face. She saw an eagerness to impress and a kind of puffing up. He wasn't shaking branches, bristling his hair and charging around, but it was clear to her he was engaged in some form of display. She looked around the room and saw everyone suddenly as an ape, and thought abruptly of all human communication as a form of grooming or dominance display.

"They were primarily fruit-eaters which is interesting symbolically." Matthew was still talking. "Lucy wouldn't accept a low status, a status that prevented her from eating the most prized fruit—the fruit of the tree of knowledge of good and evil. So she branched out on her own and ate whatever fruit she wanted, taking her mate with her. Here, have a bite of my apple. They started a new species."

"We have enough trouble with the creationists without moving into that kind of territory," Frank said. "Besides, I'd like to avoid too literal a story for the display."

"The key is the gaze," Margaret murmured, then had to elaborate. "Eye contact. That's why people go to zoos. To look in the eyes of animals: of dangerous predators, cold-blooded reptiles, apes and whales. To feel a connection, like they're communicating with the animals. 'Eyes are the windows of consciousness.'"

"Yeah," agreed Matthew. "Eye contact. If the australopithecines are too involved in their own action it will have a distancing effect for the audience."

"I suppose, you know, that's what's really happening," Neill commented slowly. "The australopithecines are standing in a museum in front of a strange new species. They've been catapulted from their past into our present. And the visitors are staring into the face of their own past. I guess both creatures might be staring out at the visitors, with expressions of wonder and curiosity."

"Close encounters of the prehistoric kind?" said Frank.

"As though just at the moment the footprints are being made," Margaret said quietly, "time collapses for a second and the creatures hear a sound from the future."

"I like the understatement of focusing on the gaze," said Frank. "I think that could be powerful. Unusual and simple."

"I still need some notion of a backstory," said Neill. "What's he doing there? He can be listening, gazing, looking, sure, but why is he standing in that particular spot at that particular time? I'd like to include a hint of challenge in the male's expression, a hint of territoriality and protectiveness."

As Neill drove Margaret home she remembered her father impatiently and disdainfully commenting on how people talked too much, how they loved the sound of their own voices, how they went on and on about nothing. She remembered the comment because, as the most talkative member of their family, she'd thought it included her and she'd been hurt. But her father had missed the point.

People frequently didn't talk for content, they were

actually using language as a replacement for touching, for patting each other, picking insects and ticks and flakes of skin out of each other's fur, comforting and reassuring each other and reaffirming their kinship and friendship bonds. *Hello, how are you? I'm fine, how're you? Nice weather today. Yeah it's beautiful, a little chilly though. How's Fred?* and so on. Language as grooming. For some reason the thought was comforting. Perhaps because, for Margaret, it added a layer of meaning to words.

Margaret put down the large chisel and mallet she was using for roughing out a large piece of black streaky marble that measured roughly three feet by two feet by two feet. She could feel the sculpture inside—nascent, existing already in a pre-concrete limbo. After her years of paralysis, working with stone again felt like pushing off into white-water rapids, or climbing the sheer side of a mountain. Adrenalin was released into her bloodstream even before she picked up her chisel. A whirlpool of pent-up energy drew her up in a manic spiral.

Afterwards she was exhausted. She sat down in her armchair, had a short nap, then turned to the reconstruction. Today was the jugular vein, the carotid artery and the esophagus. She'd found blue plastic tubing for the carotid, red tubing for the jugular, some of which she'd sent over to Neill for the male, and clear plastic tubing for the esophagus. She'd even found Neill a slightly wider tube for the male's esophagus. She attached hers inside the skull with pins and glue.

They were not essential but she thought they'd help orient her functionally to the body, help draw her down from the head to the body, help animate the clay for her and conjure up the warmth of Lucy's body. They might remind her that the creature she was building was made up mostly of fluid, not clay, and needed continual circulation. They might remind her Lucy had a pulse.

She hated feeling her own pulse. The few times she'd tried she'd dropped her wrist in revulsion after the second or third throb as though she'd unwittingly picked up a wriggling snake. The involuntary movement felt so foreign, as though her heart were a separate creature with a life of its own inhabiting her body.

Her pulse made her feel the way she imagined a hemophiliac did when he felt his own pulse. If a puncture should appear somewhere in her skin, a cut or scrape, surely each heartbeat would push volumes of blood out. She found it hard to trust that blood would eventually clot. Coagulation and clotting seemed a feeble protection against the leaking out of one's lifeblood. And she was superstitious. A watched kettle. As though feeling her pulse might cause her heart to stop beating.

She preferred to think of her body being like Lucy's: immutable clay, dependent only on gravity and the electrical charges that held molecules together. Or she liked the notion of her body as a vessel through which things flowed, light, water, earth, sound, air. She did not like the image of a red squirming muscle, flopping madly about inside her rib cage, despotically holding the rest of her body to ransom.

TWENTY

F ind the vein, snaking through solid mass, branching into myriad pathways, which fork and branch and so on until, ah-ha!

Nothing.

Find the fault, the weak point where oneness can be pried into two and two. *Tap, tap*, like someone knocking unobtrusively on a door, and you *are* knocking on a door, mallet and chisel in hand. *Tap, tap*. Stone flakes as though it had always been destined to separate at just that point; as though when it formed eons ago, on that day when it still belonged to a large mass and veins shot through the boiling magma, at just that moment when the whole thing began to cool and freeze its pattern of branching veins, certain sections cohered more completely than others and the fault lines you are prying loose today were created.

And here you stand eons later, chisel and mallet in hand, tap-tapping, looking in your white smock like an angel of masonry; you search out the fault and insinuate your tool and coax the stone to become two, and two, and two. What for? Another oneness hidden inside, a oneness for which this oneness is just a covering. Unlock the voice of the past, strike it like a Jew's harp and start a resonance. You listen for this sound, the stone's voice, as you trace the vein like a melody leading through the matter to the heart.

She washed the stone dust off her hands. It was so fine the slightest breeze carried it into crevices and onto any available surface in the room. Several years ago, when she'd been doing a lot of sculpting, the house would sometimes be blanketed with a thin film of the stuff. John hated it. He'd tried to insulate her studio by covering the vents and the outside of the door with plastic sheeting, but somehow it still found its way into every room. He used to scold her about the hazards of breathing it in. "Wear a mask for God's sake when you work," and "God knows what you're doing to my lungs letting this stuff drift through the house."

She herself wondered if she was trying to turn herself to stone, she breathed so much in. Why didn't she wear a mask? The truth was she liked the idea of stone dust lining her lungs, her throat, stomach, intestines. It gave her a sense of protection, insulation. She wanted to embody the completeness of stone and its impermeability. She wanted to feel no pain, no fear, no decay.

She ate lunch and went back to the studio to start the day's work on the reconstruction. A few days earlier she'd begun work on the left hand and lower arm. She'd made an interosseous membrane out of latex to join the radius and ulna. Some of the hand muscles were continuations of arm muscles so she'd worked first attaching the muscles of the forearm. She formed the flexor profundis digitorum, which was a tricky one because it divided into four tendons that attached to the tip of each finger.

As the palm gained muscle and shape an image came to mind of a white striped hand floating, disembodied, with other white hands on a black wall. For a minute she thought she was just remembering the image from the story she'd told at her dinner party, but then she remembered that the wall was a cave wall and it was black from smoke. The image was from a prehistoric cave painting in California somewhere and she'd seen it in a book.

She went over to her bookcase, sat on the dusty floor and began pulling books out looking for the photograph. It was in the third book, a book on cave painting she'd bought at the Museum of Natural History bookstore in Washington when she was an art student. It was a two-page spread; the caption said the cave was in central California and the white paint probably came from pigment made from diatomaceous earth, "a light-coloured material composed of the shells of minute sea creatures, called diatoms." The local nursery sold it by the bag to kill slugs. When they tried to crawl across it, the microscopic edges of the shells sliced their bellies.

It was easy to see why the image had stayed with her for ten years. It was haunting and primal. Margaret leaned back against the bookcase and looked up through the window to the lower branches of the fir tree, quiet and empty in the afternoon heat.

White handfish swimming up the deep-sea wall; zebra souls reaching for heaven, snaking their limber way from the past to the present. The artists making these handprints may have thought: this will stand for me in the time to come, my sign, my name, my *logos*. Perhaps they thought forward to her eyes seeing their handprints...one mind reaching forward, one reaching back. Her mind sought to insinuate itself behind their eyes, to intuit their consciousness, to get under their skins like a shaman in a bearskin and magically become another person. They were, after all, only separated by time, time that was invisible, relative, made of light.

A hand darts out in the darkness, caught in the beam of a flashlight, places itself over the image—an encounter more intimate and sensual than a handshake, this pressing up against, informed by an unconditional desire to know. Why shouldn't this warm hand pressed up against cold blackened limestone—all senses prickling and open in this close dark womb—why, but for a whisper of time, shouldn't it intuit the consciousness of an ancient human whose hand is printed there? Why shouldn't that ancient human have intuited hers across the temporal landscape, I to I, across death, thousands of deaths, to a moment of pressing intimacy, a gaze pregnant with desire for knowledge, a moment flying past the scattering of marked and unmarked graves...to form a kind of longevity.

She remembered Phillip's hand gently holding her neck, then his fingers caressing the tender skin underneath her chin, lingering, as though touching a rose petal or translucent caterpillar, cautious not to crush it by a small clumsy or false move.

She spent the rest of the afternoon attaching the flexor profundis digitorum and beginning to shape the flexor brevis pollicis, the fleshy round muscle in the cushion of the palm below the thumb. At five-thirty, when the late-afternoon heat and the pollution of rush hour made the air heavy and thick and her muscles needed a break from fine motor movement, she went out into the garden.

Outside she was still alone but she didn't feel so isolated: the sounds from the street and the clatter of her neighbours' dishes through their kitchen windows, their murmurs back and forth, even the less agreeable sounds of their televisions and radios comforted her.

Last week the local nursery had put their perennials on sale and she'd splurged. Two plastic trays in the shade of the apple tree were loaded with delphiniums, lupins, a clematis vine, poppies, shasta daisies, black-eyed Susans, foxgloves. They were all getting ragged and spindly and needed to be planted. But she didn't feel like planting, she wanted to dig. She wanted to finish a new kidney-shaped island flowerbed she'd started in the middle of a section of lawn to the left of the garden path. She was driven by curiosity, by a sense that something else might lie hidden under the earth in her backyard. Something she was meant to find.

She dug out the middle part of the kidney-shaped bed, prying up turf, sifting out clumps of roots and the larger stones, then loaded the turf into a wheelbarrow and wheeled it to the back fence to add to a pile already a foot high and four feet long. She carried two bags of steer manure from the garage, one for the tomato bed in the corner and the other for a round island flowerbed she'd made to the right of the path and behind the apple tree. The dark manure made the soil seem fertile and rich, as though anything planted there would soon burst out in giant blossoms.

First she planted the foxgloves along the back of the tomato bed. Then she arranged the daisies, black-eyed Susans and red poppies on the round bed. As she squatted to dig holes for the flowers, she was aware of Lucy inside her, squatting too, holding not a trowel but rather a short, thick digging stick. Lucy was digging in the earth for grubs, larvae, worms, beetles. The thumb felt short and more awkward with the stick than her human hand did with the trowel; Lucy's movements were slow and deliberate.

Digging was imprinted in her brain and bound up with her senses: the smell of freshly broken earth, her eyes scanning for insects trying to reburrow into their disturbed environment, plucking a wriggling beetle up between thumb and forefinger, pop! into the mouth. Margaret stopped at that thought and pried a daisy out of its pot. The roots had grown round the inside of the pot and were poking out of all the drainage holes so, to avoid damaging the root ball, she broke the plastic open. She placed the square-shaped nest of roots into the hole, poured water in and packed wet dirt firmly around it.

These motions would have been foreign to Lucy. She wouldn't have known the satisfaction of planting something with roots, or the pleasure of imagining the roots drinking in nutrients and water below so the plant on the surface can form buds that will expand and open out into flowers whose colour your eye will drink in like velvet, like the softness of a lake, like the infinity of blue sky. Your eye will look and look and look until it is saturated with the pure colour of the flower. Its pollen will travel with bees and become honey. The flower will hide earwigs; it will feed aphids masochistically, unsymbiotically. And you will follow the destiny of the flower and what happens to the flower will matter to you.

But for Lucy it was not the eye consuming but the mouth, the nose, the ears. All the senses balanced and connected to a kinesthetic sense, her body here and now, where Margaret's body always seemed to have one foot in the future and the other sunk into the past.

She dug a hole for a black-eyed Susan and turned up a fat amber-coloured case with a larva of some sort curled inside. For a moment she felt an urge to pop it into her mouth and give Lucy something to eat. But Lucy wasn't hungry. She was being fed with blood and oxygen like a foetus.

You chisel out the eyes. It's the only way to make them see. They are covered by shards. A straight sharp blade hammered at the right place and right angle will knock the detritus off like scales. Fish scales. Stone scales.

Streaked with white veins, covered by a film of stone dust, the true lustre of the eyes will remain hidden until they are sanded with wet sandpaper. A jutting brow shades their burning recess but still you can see them, you can see desire arising from death, desire that can be met only fleetingly, a dark buzz, a drone of loss, an emptiness in the heart, the loss of love, its departure so much more ripping and tearing than simple absence.

Eyes stripped clean of scales, so that they are raw and naked and cannot conceal the pain that is bound to desire, like Siamese twins—pain, desire—sharing a heart.

See, see! See the world! But the expressiveness of these eyes is too forceful. In that sense they are self-absorbed. You can see in, but they don't see out. The scales have been scraped off only so you can see in. They remain unchanged.

TWENTY-ONE

Over the next three weeks Margaret left the house only for visits to the dentist and trips to the all-night supermarket for food and packs of bubble-gum. Whenever she worked really hard at something she liked to chew gum. She never restricted herself to one piece, she always started with a wad of a minimum of three. Helen had suggested she might be relieving sexual frustration but Margaret laughed and said it was just a simple desire to chew hard on something springy, to bite down and exercise her jaw muscles, like chimpanzees chewing on leaf wads.

She finished the left arm and hand in two weeks. Their right counterparts took only six days because, rather than doing a layered reconstruction, she sculpted them as mirror images of the left.

Neill dropped by when she was ready to start the feet.

Probably the most controversial aspect of Lucy now was her mode of locomotion. No one denied that Lucy walked erect—the controversy lay in whether this was her only mode or even her primary mode of locomotion. Someone had determined recently that Lucy's feet would have had the same relationship to her body as a human wearing big clown shoes, and so he'd videotaped a group of people walking around in the clown shoes for a few hours to prove that extended periods of erect walking would have been too cumbersome and different from the way modern people walk.

Despite the controversy Margaret and Neill quickly agreed that the anatomical decisions were fairly straightforward. The gluteal muscles, so important in bipedalism, were already oriented horizontally in Lucy, similar to those of humans, not like chimpanzees. The big toe was much closer to the other toes than a chimpanzee's, and the toes were also all substantially shorter. Margaret thought, for example, it might be unlikely afarensis babies could have clung to their mother's fur for very long and probably would have had to be carried.

Margaret and Neill also both tended to think bipedal walking was afarensis's primary mode of locomotion, based on the skeletal evidence alone. However they thought Lucy might well have spent some time in trees gathering fruit or avoiding predators and may even have slept in trees at night. They discussed small questions of emphasis: just how powerful would they render the arm muscles, how hunched the shoulders, how limber and curved the toes?

Margaret enjoyed working on the powerful leg muscles. As she attached the most superficial calf muscle, gastrocnemius, used to push the front of the foot down on the ground and propel the body forward, it occurred to her that she knew Lucy's muscles, tendons and bones better than her own. She knew the size, shape, texture and attachment of every muscle. Even when she'd studied human anatomy and helped with a dissection she hadn't actually formed each muscle and attached it.

The volume and mass of each muscle of Lucy's body was imprinted in her memory in a three-dimensional image. And her own muscles twitched in recognition, in a muscle memory of movement, with an echoing motion of their own. She thought this intimate knowledge might explain the sensation she had of Lucy coalescing and coming alive inside her, the sense she had of a smaller body making minimal, precise, darting movements inside hers.

As she worked now she often practised chimpanzee calls, trying out slight variations she thought might lead to equivalent human sounds. Mostly she practised the quieter sounds: soft pant-grunts, whimpers, squeaks, soft barks, the soft *huu* of puzzlement.

Human language was governed by the brain's neocortex, while chimpanzee sound production, and human emotive sounds like screams and cries, were governed by the limbic system, also referred to as the "visceral" brain. This was the same part of the brain that regulated heart and respiration rates, hormone levels and facial expressions. It also played a part in attention, motivation and arousal. Since Lucy's brain size was about the same as a chimpanzee's, her sound production was also likely governed by the limbic system.

Margaret found herself drifting in a marine environment of emotional currents, none attached to anything real. She chattered and grunted and chuckled and smacked her lips and occasionally, during the day when she hoped that the sounds of traffic and lawn mowers and children would mask them, she practised pant-hoots and screams.

After finishing the limbs she worked on the pelvic area and the inner organs. She left the abdomen unfinished because she was unsure of the position and depth of the umbilicus, and at the time she didn't feel like talking to Neill again. She reconstructed Lucy's shoulder and back muscles, and by the end of July she was ready to work on the chest.

The work on the reconstruction continued to go smoothly and steadily. Aside from her trips to the dentist and the supermarket, she interrupted her work only for gardening—usually digging a new flowerbed or planting something interesting she'd picked up at the nursery. Or she worked on her sculpture.

Often over this period she left her phone unplugged, so Neill contacted her by mail when he needed to speak to her and arranged for her to phone him back at specific times. He was quite tolerant of her antisocial behaviour and her need for isolation. During a phone call at the end of July he reminded her of a formal dinner organized by the museum's fund-raising committee for August 13. He emphasized how important it was that she be there. Part of the evening's program was for a member of the Human Origins Committee to be present at each table of patrons to answer questions and talk about recent discoveries and controversies.

She wondered out loud what would happen if she

were sick. Neill said unless she was actually going to vomit at the table she should probably attend.

She spoke with Neill again on August 7, just after she'd finished reconstructing Lucy's pectoral muscles and breasts. Again he reminded her of the fund-raiser and explained that she would need a fairly formal dress. She asked him why he kept mentioning it.

"Well Margaret, I suppose I feel the need to remind you again because you seem, and coming from me you'll understand how extreme it must be, you seem very pre-occupied with your work. You live alone, you unplug your telephone, you can't be seeing people much because no one would be able to reach you, so it just seems likely that Saturday will come and go and you won't necessarily even notice that it's August 13 and even if you do it won't occur to you that you have an event to attend."

After she hung up she thought that actually she was sort of looking forward to the evening now that it was only a week away. She was almost ready to come out of hiding.

She forgot to unplug the phone again and a few hours later it rang. She answered, feeling reckless and a little curious.

It was June phoning to invite her to dinner. Margaret thanked her but said she really couldn't until the recon-struction was finished. The deadline was just too tight.

"Why don't you have your answering-machine on any more? It's impossible to reach you."

"I know, I'm sorry. It's broken," she lied. "I have to get a new message tape and I just haven't got around to it."

"Yeah, sure," June said somewhat aggressively.

Margaret let out a short grunt of irritation in reply.

Really she couldn't think of anything to say, and the grunt expressed her feelings more accurately than any words would have. She said goodbye in as pleasant and friendly a manner as possible and hung up.

She guessed the grunt had been a mistake when a few hours later there was a knock on her door and it was David, who said he and June had just been talking to Helen on the phone and they were quite concerned about her.

"You're under a lot of stress right now with the divorce and your teeth and your money situation," he said, leaning in the doorway to her kitchen scrutinizing her as she put the kettle on for tea. "Frankly I think you could ask John to help you out there. Anyway, you're working all the time and isolating yourself completely. I mean, look here, at this room," he called from the doorway to her studio. "You're surrounded by bones and skulls and you spend all your time here, working on this." David pointed to the reconstruction. "That thing looks horrific."

She supposed it did. Its eyes seemed to bug out in terror and its body looked like a skinned rabbit, half-dissected, all its muscles and tendons bared immodestly, roughly formed organs visible between the deep muscles in the abdominal cavity—yes, she supposed absent-mindedly, it could look horrific if you wanted to look at it that way.

"I don't just work on the reconstruction. I read a lot too. And see over there. I've started a new sculpture. Finally, after three years."

"You need to get out, Margaret. See people. Get a reality check once in a while. Treat yourself a little.

Don't be so hard on yourself."

"I *am* going out soon. Next weekend in fact. There's a fund-raising banquet for the Human Origins Hall. Black tie and a five-course meal. There'll be lots of people." She felt like a child making excuses to a parent.

"David, I know you're here out of concern, but I'm fine."

"You seem odd, Margaret. I mean, look at the way you're dressed—like you slept in those clothes for the last week. You need to take care of yourself. There are hairy things growing in your kitchen."

"There have been hairy things growing in my kitchen for the last five years. You just haven't noticed. And I often sleep in my clothes."

"I don't know. I don't mean to be critical. You just seem absent somehow."

She felt suddenly lucky in her friends. She was surprised they would care if she wasn't doing well. She always assumed that if she wasn't cheerful and strong, if she didn't have something to offer, no one would want anything to do with her. She didn't actually believe that friendship and love were anything more than very sophisticated, complex emotional barter systems. When she was depressed she often felt scared because she knew she had nothing to trade for love.

She thanked David for his concern and made a pot of coffee. She promised him she'd make an effort to call him or Helen or June periodically to touch base. He stayed for a couple of hours and they talked about movies he'd seen, about the problem of June's growing bitterness and frustration and about Helen's funny brilliance and their hopes for outrageous success for her in the academic world. And Margaret told David a bit about the sculpture she was working on.

"I haven't felt this excited about anything since art school."

The hairdresser's was a half-hour walk from Margaret's house. She had a nine o'clock appointment on a Sunday morning so the streets were pretty empty, and she found herself letting Lucy take over her gait. Her stride became shorter and her legs felt farther apart, making her look a bit like a cowboy just out of the saddle. She rolled more from side to side, exaggerating the shift in weight from one foot to the other. Her hands curled and her third-finger joints brushed her thighs as she advanced. She didn't swing her arms when she walked, instead they hung down straighter from the shoulder. Her feet turned outward when she walked and her longer toes felt more dextrous. She became hyper-aware of her big toe, and the gap between it and the rest of her toes seemed to increase somewhat. Her head jutted forward and by the time she reached the main street where the hairdresser's was located her neck muscles were strained and aching.

She saw her posture in the plate-glass window of a Turkish carpet store. She looked a bit like a cross between a sullen, goofy teenager and a chimpanzee—not quite one or the other, but something unique; something that her human body could not really articulate. A man in a suit looked back at her through her reflection from inside the store. He smiled and nodded. She smiled back, shook her shoulders, resumed her normal gait and strode into grooming heaven.

At Sasha's Salon they included a shiatsu scalp massage in the ritual of washing and conditioning their patrons' hair, and Margaret was led to her hairdresser Michael's chair in a state of passive bliss. He arrived in a fading waft of cigarette smoke, looked at her in the mirror, played lightly with her hair and asked what she would like done. She shivered because as he touched her hair she realized no one had touched her for months.

Two opposite banks of mirrors enabled customers to see everyone sitting behind them, as well as the backs of the heads of people beside them, in images that repeated *ad infinitum.* Margaret particularly liked watching people staring at themselves. It seemed to her they were trying to make their own faces familiar, trying to reconcile the slightly jarring image in the mirror with their inner sense of how they looked.

She stared at a woman a few chairs down who was wincing as her hairdresser used a hook to pull strands of hair through holes in a plastic cap. The woman noticed her looking and glared back with a stony frown. Margaret quickly averted her gaze to someone else, then checked back to see if the woman was still staring at her. She was. Margaret kept checking until at last the woman was looking somewhere else.

It was one thing to stare when the other person wasn't looking, but staring at someone who was looking back was a whole different matter. For gorillas and chimpanzees a stare was either an aggressive threat or indicated a desire to copulate. In the former situation subordinates quickly averted their eyes, usually downward, and moved away.

"It's not polite to stare," her mother used to whisper

when her daughter would fix someone in her gaze on a bus or in the supermarket. Probably for humans it was still aggressive behaviour. Or the second category. Phillip had stared at her that day in the museum and she hadn't felt threatened at all. She remembered wanting to laugh. But that was probably because, though she didn't know it at the time, she was sexually available. And of course because she thought he was so handsome.

That following week, the second week in August, she began work on the last part of the reconstruction, the neck. She was really looking forward to reconstructing the neck because it would bring the body, which was more or less complete, into continuity with the head. She phoned David and spoke briefly with him, then went back to work. She realized quite by surprise that she wasn't lonely any more. And the dull roar of frustration and pain in her background consciousness (perhaps pain was too grandiose a word—discomfort was better) was fading. A concentrated stillness was taking its place. The ravenous, snapping jaws that had been the self feeding on the self for so long were being replaced by the alert, small, compact form of Lucy, who approached slowly, hesitantly, with a gaze that wondered benignly who Margaret might be.

She enjoyed being alone, watching thoughts pass through her mind. It no longer made her anxious that they went unuttered and unwitnessed before they passed out into infinite nothingness. She liked her life—puttering around in her garden, working on her sculpture, and feeling Lucy gradually becoming whole under her fingertips.

TWENTY-TWO

The boutique is a small cubbyhole with new clothes hanging from every available surface. All the fabrics are rich and bright: sequined, embroidered, beaded velvet, satin, edged with piping or lace. Costumes in some sense, but also everyday clothes. It's like being in a burrow lined with gleaming cloth—the walls and ceiling are hard brown earth. She wonders if the store has problems with mice and rats making nests in the clothes, but nothing touches the floor and there are no shelves or drawers. Even the pantyhose are displayed on hangers.

She is stealing time. She should be back at work. Her boss will be furious if he finds outs, but she just can't quite tear herself away. She wanders in further. She's hoping to find something wonderful, something that will change her into a princess. But she doesn't think princess, she thinks—beautiful, new. She eases a pair of bright-green velvet pants with covered buttons out of the tight pack of clothes on a rack. They're a style she loves and has seen on other women; they have a front panel that buttons up over the hips like a sailor's. She tries them on, feeling excited, but they end an inch above her ankles.

"Oh they're perfect! You have the right figure for them," the saleswoman exclaims. Margaret wishes she could believe her.

She asks for the next size up, and these are the right length, but they're much too wide.

"They're pedal-pushers," the saleswoman lies. "They're supposed to be short." She hates pedal-pushers. They seem out of proportion. They make her feel like a child or a housewife from the fifties.

She glances anxiously at her watch but doesn't register the time. Before she can check again she notices sale tickets on everything. A shiny green-and-gold minidress, sixties style, hangs from the ceiling. It's sleeveless with a zipper up the back. When she tries the dress on it puckers behind the arms and billows at the waist and makes her body look blocky. Her legs, however, look really sexy in it and this makes her want to buy it. Now she wants to buy the pants too.

She checks her watch again. Two hours have gone by. *How could I do this?* she asks herself, panicking, and starts putting her old clothes back on.

She leaves feeling she'll never look beautiful; she'll never find anything that fits right. She wonders if this is a flaw in her or in clothes designers or if she just needs to spend more time looking. It seems like it should be possible for her to find the right clothes, she just hasn't found the key yet and she never seems to have time to look. But it's very important.

TWENTY-THREE

At four o'clock the day before the fund-raising banquet Margaret stopped work and had a hot bath. In the bath she began to wonder what to wear. She remembered her dream and it occurred to her that it might be difficult to find something. She'd bought a beautiful dress five years ago for John's graduation party but it was floor-length and too formal. Since then they'd rarely gone out. John had borrowed money to buy a medical practice and he'd wanted to pay off that loan and his student loan as fast as possible, so he never wanted to spend money on restaurants or vacations. Occasionally a professor who'd taken an interest in him invited them over for dinner and she wore her only pair of dress pants. Just as John finished paying off his loans they stopped doing anything together. For the last two years she hadn't really worn anything but jeans and sweaters or T-shirts.

She climbed out of the tub and left wet footprints as she went upstairs to take inventory of her closet. Her dress pants had been worn so often they'd lost their shape and the knees were shiny. And that was it, except for her great-aunt's muu-muu and a large soft plastic box zipped around ten hangers at the back of the closet. These were clothes she'd inherited from her mother. She had a vague idea what was inside but she hadn't looked since just after the death. She unzipped it. Four skirt-and-sweater sets in moss green, bright pink, navy and cream, two nubbly wool suits, three wool shirt-dresses from Scotland in soft earthy tones and one basic black dress with short sleeves and a plain round neck.

She tried on the black dress. The darts were made for a larger-breasted woman and the wool puckered slightly there but a padded bra would probably solve the problem. She rummaged through her shoes and found a pair of black suede pumps. If she took the hem up above the knee and found the right piece of jewellery, the dress might look quite elegant.

The next day she bought a lightly padded black bra with matching underwear, raised the hem of the dress and ironed it. Everything took longer than she'd anticipated so, to save time, she phoned for a taxi before she was finished dressing. The driver honked his horn just as she was pulling up her stockings. She yanked them too hard and poked her finger through the nylon. A run slithered quickly down to her ankle. She waved to him out the window and hurriedly cauterized the run at either end with red nail polish, threw her lipstick into her purse to put on later and clattered down the front stairs. She got the driver to stop outside a large drugstore while she ran in and bought a new pair of stockings.

She changed in the ladies' room just off the hotel lobby. The walls were sponged a creamy yellow, the floor was covered with terracotta tile and the countertops were marble. There was a powder room with two deep armchairs upholstered in heavy polished cotton. Several prints hung on the walls, for the most part depicting the usual flaxen-haired girls in summer gardens or on picnics, but one caught her eye. It was of a small ocean bay with killer whales cavorting in the mist. A grey-haired woman in loose khaki shorts and a white shirt watched from a hill.

The vanity had a porcelain bowl filled with packaged towelettes. Margaret sat down in front of the mirror and took more care than usual with her lipstick. She thought of her dream of the gangster boss and the perfect makeup and gazing into the tiny compact mirror in the back seat of his immaculate car. In a way this lounge reminded her of that car in its perfect order and luxuriousness. Perfection in that dream had been about order: the boss's, which was fascistic and about control; and the order involved in painting her face, creating something under duress to continue past her death. It was that small order-making, coupled with the singer touching her naked, warm, sun-tanned breasts, that had created the feeling of freedom and liberation in her dream.

She stood back to survey herself. She'd achieved the necessary transformation. She looked elegant in a plain way. Maybe even beautiful.

At the reception desk she was directed to the Rosetti Banquet Hall. It was huge and decorated in a modern, restrained interpretation of rococo: gilt-scrolled mouldings, chandeliers, rosy pink carpet with gold and ivory curlicues. A row of about twenty waiters in black tuxedos stood silently against the wall. One of them stepped out from the row and took her coat and cocktail order. He returned with drink and hat-check number held aloft on a tray, then dissolved back into the silent row.

Most of the guests had gathered in small clusters near the far wall by a table with an enormous floral centrepiece and trays of canapés and other hors d'oeuvres. Margaret spied Frank holding forth to one such cluster and she walked past the waiters toward him. She felt that everyone was looking at her and that no one was. She felt attractive one moment and awkwardly flawed the next, wanting to be looked at but also wanting to hide under a table.

Frank smiled at her when she reached his group. She stood beside him waiting while he finished talking to a silver-haired man. The man and his companion glanced inquiringly at her.

As usual Frank spoke voluminously and she began to feel embarrassed waiting silently. She didn't know what to do with her eyes or her hands, what facial expression to adopt. She noticed the silver-haired man glancing out of the corner of his eye in the direction of her feet several times and she began to wonder what attracted his attention. She stared at the floral arrangement. She imagined Frank following the man's glance and then the woman and a look of alarm and discomfort developing on their faces. They would begin to inch away, rotating away from her, dissociating themselves publicly from her.

She would glance down nonchalantly at her feet to see what they were looking at. A pair of furry chimpanzee legs and large hairy feet would protrude from below the hem of her dress. She'd want to flee, but she wouldn't know how to get across the hall without everyone seeing her legs. She'd be frozen, just as she was now, exposed, nowhere to hide.

A soft gong sounded and people gravitated toward the dinner tables. Frank took Margaret's arm, helped the guests find their places and then showed her to her seat. Each setting had three silver forks, three knives, a soup spoon and two teaspoons, a large dinner plate, salad plate, soup bowl and bread plate in a simple pattern of cream and gold-leaf, two crystal wine glasses, a champagne flute, and a name-card printed on both sides.

Frank introduced Margaret to a couple already seated at the table. They smiled and offered their names, Drs. Joe and Sandy Morris. He had a compact, powerful build, dark hair and penetrating brown eyes, while she had a tall, willowy build, light brown hair and a slightly distracted look in her blue eyes. Frank briefly described the work Margaret did for the museum and left.

Another couple approached. The husband was in his late forties and wore a well-made black suit, crisp white shirt, conventional tie. He located their name-cards and introduced himself and his wife as Albert and Sharon Johnson. Her age was difficult to guess because she had a childlike face and she looked as though she'd never lost her baby-fat. Her complexion was peachy and fair. As she was introduced she looked at everyone with a disarmingly direct innocence.

They sat down. The husband fidgeted nervously with his name-card while his wife stared just above people's heads with a vague, small smile.

A woman in a floor-length embroidered Mexican

wedding dress read out one of the last two unclaimed cards. "Mrs. B. Buchbinder. Here we are, Bob," she called to a man a few tables away.

"Hello everyone. I'm Betsy." She had intelligent brown eyes and a radiant smile. "I didn't marry the dear man for his last name, which I love in itself—the binder of books—but Bob and Betsy Buchbinder is a bit much."

She looked intently at each person's face as they introduced themselves. When her husband joined her she was able to introduce him to everyone at the table by name.

Frank stepped up to the podium and explained that he would be speaking after dinner but he wanted to welcome everyone and thank them for their support. "The displays and artifacts in the new Hall of Human Origins will ignite in our visitors a curiosity about their past and make them want to trace the pattern of their origins. When they do, they will discover how profoundly our species is connected with the rest of the natural world. We arise from it. We will sink back into it. If the Hall of Human Origins can affect people's consciousness of their place in the world, now when the natural world is so precarious, we will have begun to change the world. Drop one stone in a lake, ripples flow outward forever. We thank you for your generous support."

He finished by inviting the guests to feast their senses. "By the way," he added, "save your bones. We might need them for display cases if we fall short of funds!" A wave of chuckles went through the crowd.

The waiters served champagne and a wild mushroom salad. They moved quickly; Margaret was conscious of the sound of accelerating air as they passed, and the subtle hiss of pant leg against pant leg, jacket lining against shirt. Then they marched through the hall holding silver soup tureens aloft. They stood poised at each table until all were in position, then they lowered the tureens simultaneously. There were two waiters with two silver tureens at Margaret's table.

"We keep kosher," Mrs. Buchbinder explained. "Not at an Orthodox level or we wouldn't even be here, but frogs' leg soup is definitely off our list."

Margaret looked down at her curried frogs' leg soup and envied the simple vegetable broth being ladled into the Buchbinders' bowls.

"Now," Mrs. Buchbinder addressed Margaret, "what's your field? It must be so interesting to work in a museum. History is *such* an important subject."

Margaret described the Laetoli footprints to the guests and explained that they were the basis of the display she and her supervisor Neill Hansen were working on. Then she began talking about Lucy.

"The Lucy fossils were a very significant find because Lucy's brain was barely larger than a chimpanzee's yet she already walked erect. Which was incredible because everyone had always thought that the big brain came first and that that was what distinguished us as human. Not so. It was our bodies.

"All the basic anatomical changes for erect walking had already taken place. From the neck up, though, she was really different. Her brow was ridged, her jaw jutted forward, and the muscles of her jaw and neck were extremely powerful. Her teeth were large and flat. Her ears were high on her head and further back. Her nose probably did not project at all."

"Lucy is that find a few years ago in Ethiopia, isn't

it?" Joe Morris asked. "The Leakeys found it."

"That's right, although actually it was Donald Johanson who found Lucy."

"Do you enjoy your work?" Mrs. Buchbinder asked.

"Yes...very much. It's interesting to create a body that's so different from your own yet so deeply connected. When I reconstruct an arm or leg, or a part of her face, I feel reverberations in my own body. I think about her all the time, wondering what it felt like to be her, how the world looked through her eyes."

Margaret heard herself holding forth and realized that she found it easy to talk about Lucy. Especially after a couple of glasses of wine.

"Of course the only way you can really discover something like that is by studying humans and the great apes that are still alive today. When I was reading about them I was amazed how similar we are to chimpanzees and gorillas in our fundamental response to the world. There's the same exuberance. The same shyness. And loneliness.

"As an aside, you might already know this but we share 98 percent of our genetic make-up with chimpanzees. We can even accept a blood transfusion from them once if the blood types are matched. Anyway, we share the same basic anxiety and territoriality. Also the underpinnings of our societies. Not structural so much as the emotional underpinnings—the emotional experience of reality that drives us, and makes it inevitable in some ways for us to create certain social structures. Family. Teams. Business hierarchies."

Mrs. Buchbinder was the only one at the table still really listening. The others were looking around the room or toying with their cutlery.

The waiters removed the soup bowls and champagne flutes and brought a butter lettuce salad with orange slices, pecans and thin slivers of red onion. The inside set of wine glasses were filled with a German Moselle.

"Louis Leakey was the one who realized the urgent need to study surviving great apes before they became extinct. He recruited Jane Goodall to study chimpanzees, Dian Fossey for gorillas and Birute Galdikas for the orangutan. During Goodall's research she observed that it was important to the well-being and even survival of an individual chimp to be able to understand and antici-pate the behaviour of other chimps in the band. In other words, to think politically. Now anthropologists are beginning to think that this was the driving force behind the selection for bigger and bigger brains. It was social competition within the species, not with other predators, that drove the evolution of the big brain. I find this remarkable that it should have been internally driven."

The next course was guinea fowl stuffed with wild rice and pine nuts with a glacé sauce, and again, as she sucked small flakes of meat off the tiny bird's drumstick, Margaret envied the Buchbinders' halibut steaks with black butter and parsley and new potatoes. The waiters removed the white wine glasses and poured a French Beaujolais into the last wine glass.

Before working on the reconstruction Margaret had always thought of life as a thin veil over an infinite void that was death. Nothingness was the driving force of the universe. Now, as she watched the ruby liquid fill her glass, she realized she no longer believed this. Matter and energy had too many manifestations. There were too many amoebas and viruses, stalagtites, amethysts, ferns and orchids, peacocks, giraffes, pink dolphins, praying mantises, Venus flytraps, museums, images, stories, books. She'd been projecting the nothing she felt inside herself onto the universe.

Sharon Johnson dabbed her mouth carefully with her napkin as the waiters whisked away their dinner plates. She flushed as she prepared to speak.

"You people believe in evolution, then," she said.

Her husband frowned. Everyone at the table was quiet for a moment. A few eyes darted to a small gold cross she wore over her dress.

"Shut up," her husband said.

"Well yes," said Mrs. Buchbinder gently. "I do. I believe evolution is a wonderful story written by God."

Margaret stood up and excused herself from the table. She discovered she had to concentrate on not stumbling as she walked to the washroom and her eyes weren't focusing very quickly. She was drunk.

The doors to all the cubicles were closed so she peered underneath to find one without ankles and feet. They were all empty. It was a relief to sit down and stop moving. The cubicle walls shifted horizontally, vertically, a cubist painting in motion.

She stared at her feet and noticed how the shape of her shoe transformed her foot into a smooth whole, without toes or toenails or bumps or ridges, how the shoe was designed to mask any structural similarities between feet and hands. The shoe said: this foot is something to stand on, nothing else. It never grasped the branches of trees or held fruit between its toes, or tickled and tussled with babies.

Believe in evolution? She'd never asked herself the question. It seemed like asking if you believed in the existence of an ear of corn or that the earth was round. Yet the idea that living creatures metamorphosed from one thing to another over time *was* an extremely strange notion. It made her look at her hand and think, this was a fin, or perhaps an unusual fishy arm that helped an ancestral "fish" hump herself up onto a piece of wood or some dried mud to breathe air when there wasn't enough oxygen underwater. It meant believing that what were now her feet had once had long gripping toes like a chimpanzee's. Before that, they'd been paws. And before that, fins. And before that, amoebic projections. And before that?

How many detailed mutations would have to occur to change a paw into a hand, for example? Toes would have to lengthen to fingers, claws would have to recede and flatten into fingernails, the padded cushions on the underside widen out into palms, the thumb rotate to the side, and every separate muscle, ligament, bone, piece of skin, would have to alter too in a consistent way. Each mutation must be able to be passed on genetically…and this was just the hand. On examination, the idea of evolution seemed not only far-fetched but even implausible.

"When you think about it, evolution is a pretty wild idea," Margaret said after she returned to her seat. Her tongue felt thick and unwieldly and she decided to stick to water for the rest of the evening. "It's like combining surrealism and science."

Mrs. Johnson looked at her nervously, apologetically. Her husband was rigid with anger. Everyone else was silent and Margaret realized the table had been trying to change the subject.

Presently Mrs. Buchbinder spoke. "I think life is a dream. I believe our world is as though God were dreaming it. God turns over in his sleep, perhaps mutations occur. If God wakes up perhaps the world will vanish."

The waiter set the first dessert down in front of Mr. Buchbinder. It was a frothy, buoyant apparition—white meringue shapes floating in a swirl of chocolate sauce and heavy cream, with ice cream, raspberries and clouds of whipping cream.

"Jews have a prayer before sleeping," Mrs. Buchbinder continued, "'And may it be Your will, my God and God of all who came before me, to let me lie down in peace and also awake in peace.' This is interpreted as asking that while we are sleeping and not safeguarding the existence of the world by our perception of it, that God take over for us and keep all the atoms that make up our universe in the same order until morning. In the morning we thank God again, '…Who has in mercy returned my soul to me.'"

Mr. Buchbinder closed his eyes and said irreverently, "May the atoms in my dessert preserve their order long enough for me to eat it."

By the end of dessert Margaret was still a little tipsy but she'd had two cups of coffee and she no longer had to concentrate on articulating every word. The conversation at her table had broken into smaller conversations—Mrs. Buchbinder and Mrs. Johnson talked about their religions, agreeing about everything on the surface, in a social way, but really each talking in her own very separate world. The two doctors and Mr. Buchbinder discussed the museum's financial situation and Mr.

Johnson appeared to listen to them while really listening to his wife with pressurized irritation.

Margaret didn't talk any more and she only half listened as she began to retreat into her Laetoli day-dream. When Frank took the podium again and tapped his water glass with a knife to get everyone's attention, she closed her eyes, and ash drifted, lighter and softer than snow inside her eyelids, hiding a tropical world under its opaque veil. For a moment the world was made up only of ash—ash trees, ash fruit, ash sky and ash ground, ash apes, ash tablecloths, ash dessert, ash wine, ash Frank, everything ash-coloured except the bird, which flitted about so often ash never settled on it, and Lucy's shiny brown eyes, kept moist and clear by the blinking of her eyelids.

She looked up. Ash fell from the sky like snow on a cloudy day. Grey melting into grey. She stepped once more from her house into the snow, heading for what was now only her father's house. Snow settled on her hair, her eyelashes, her cheeks, and melted into rivers that found the most direct route downward over the contours of her face. Snow would no longer melt on her mother's face. It would be her shroud.

How could the doctors have known her mother had died of a brain hemorrhage so quickly, she remembered wondering. Wouldn't they have had to do an autopsy? That would have meant her mother died early in the morning and her father called them right away to take the body. Why hadn't he called his daughter sooner? He'd waited the whole day alone in that house before calling her. She'd wanted so much to see her mother's body before its blood was replaced with preservative.

Everyone shook hands with Margaret and thanked her for an informative evening. Mrs. Buchbinder gave Margaret's hand a little squeeze and said, "I look forward to seeing the finished work, my dear."

When all the patrons had left, Frank invited the museum staff over to his table for a liqueur. The waiters stacked chairs, bundled away dirty tablecloths, turned the tables onto their sides, folded up the legs and rolled them noisily out of the hall. Everyone from the museum was in good spirits, and after they'd congratulated themselves on the success of the evening, Neill suggested they reconvene at a jazz club where a good friend of his was playing saxophone.

Margaret had drunk a brandy and she felt reckless. "I feel like dancing," she said. Neill said he thought the club had a dance-floor, though he'd never really noticed if people danced or not. Frank made apologies and went home while the rest of them piled into Neill's van.

They paid a cover charge and got their hands stamped before stepping into the smoky darkness. Neill found them a table near the back behind the dance-floor, which was large and so jammed with people they couldn't see the stage. They shouted their drink orders in the waitress's ear then sat back and listened to the band and watched people dance.

A new song started up and two women from an adjacent table jumped to their feet and coaxed the two men at the table to join them. They led the men by the hand through the tables, their bodies already marking the beat. On the dance-floor they sprang into motion and Margaret found herself marvelling at how good their pelvic bones were at keeping their digestive organs up off the floor. She thought about their femurs and tibias, held together by sheathes of ligament and cushioned by cartilege, and of the fragile foot bones, and marvelled again at how their brains co-ordinated the separate movement of so many different body parts into a dance step, a step followed by other steps to create a rhythmic pattern. And then slight nuances in all these connected movements managed to express the personality of the dancer and the emotions the music caused inside them.

She perceived how one leg prepared to support the whole weight of the body as the other lifted up. One foot gripped the floor more tightly in anticipation of being the only contact with the ground. Then the other foot lifted and the whole structure, balanced on one foot, not only didn't topple over but actually lifted itself into the air and was suspended momentarily, free of any contact with the ground. And then the landing!

She winced at the impact, the shuddering compression throughout the structure, the brief moment when the whole tinker-toy outfit might buckle and fall to the floor in a pile of bones tangled up with muscle and skin. But no—it held. The first foot made contact with the floor again with a slight bend at the knee, and the whole structure once again demonstrated its resilience, barely seeming to waver before the weight shifted to the other foot and the dancer hopped again!

The band ended the song and announced a break, and Neill went to invite his friend back to their table for a drink. Margaret was curious to see what the friend looked like. She'd distinguished the sound of the saxophone soaring over the room, reminding her of a bird aiming for the sun.

The friend was Phillip. She recognized him right away and blushed. She blushed with pleasure, but also because she had intimate images which were discordant with the fact that she barely knew him. She felt embarrassed. Then she felt distressed at not being sober.

He recognized her too and addressed her before Neill could introduce him to anyone. "I didn't know if I should try to reach you, but I wanted to."

She doubted he was listening to her answer, so direct and probing was his gaze. She was struck by the intensity of the blueness of his eyes.

It should have seemed strange, even hallucinatory, to see him again this way, but instead it just seemed normal. For Margaret, normal was the same as familiar, and her sense of familiarity was both very fragile and very elastic. Dream and reality, concrete and abstract, present and past—all tended to blend and cross over.

"I thought about you often," he said. He certainly wasn't playing his cards close to the chest. She'd noticed this earnestness before and she wondered about it. She tried to detect emotional neediness in it, but it seemed more like he'd made a decision in principle to be straightforward and direct. There was nothing strategic about him and he seemed unconcerned about what social light his directness might leave him in.

"You *know* each other?" Neill asked.

"Yes," Margaret answered. Phillip pulled a chair up between Margaret and Neill.

"Where from?" Neill asked, still standing. "We met in your museum," Phillip said. "At the Neanderthal burial site. We had a good conversation."

"When?" Neill asked.

"I really enjoyed listening to you play," Margaret intercepted Neill's questioning. "I thought the saxophone sounded like a beautiful yellow bird."

"Thank you." He smiled at her.

"Small world." Neill shrugged.

Phillip asked after her husband and she told him they were separated.

"I'm sorry."

She asked how he was doing. He said the woman he'd been living with had left him. A smile reached her lips before she could supress it.

"In a way I really hadn't been in the relationship for the last few years," he added.

Margaret was extremely aware of where her body was in relation to his body and she found it difficult to concentrate on what he was saying. Her body was having its own conversation with him, and like a young child, it kept interrupting its parents while they talked.

Neill must have ordered another round for the table because a second martini arrived in front of Margaret that she didn't remember ordering. She gulped down the rest of her first and gave the empty glass to the waitress. She was beginning to feel silly, and although she was sober enough to be aware of herself being silly, she wasn't sober enough to stop herself. When Phillip had to go back on stage she was grateful. She knew she wasn't going to stop drinking this time. Some part of her seemed impelled to finish what she'd begun. What had she begun? She wanted to be in her dark side. What dark side? She just wanted to let go, to be free from caution and worry and frustration.

Phillip found them a table closer to the stage for the

second set. Margaret watched him play. His eyes were closed and he turned his face up toward the black ceiling, as though it were the night sky and open and infinite. She imagined the storeys of hotel rooms above, each inhabitant living out his or her small parcel of time, some turning away from one another in anger and irritation and some embracing skin to skin, slippery with perspiration, feverishly trying to merge what was separate, and yet maybe not so separate after all. Like the Jack of Spades in a deck of cards, two identical faces bound forever to look away from each other.

Someone else ordered a round of draft beer for the table and she found herself sipping from a glass of beer without remembering finishing the second martini. The music surged over her and she began to feel ecstatic, overwhelmed by a kind of cosmic inclusiveness, All Things embodied in the music's rhythm and releases, an implicit hymn of thanks for everything, for every moment lived by every person.

I'm drunk, she thought. *Who cares?* Tonight she would release herself to the sky, to the strangers in the hotel rooms above her, to the thick, poignant scenes of their lives. She would be the most generous of audiences, she would abandon her fear, her loneliness, her emptiness— the tiny anxious cluster of her separate identity—and become one with the universe that was unfolding around her.

The audience broke into applause when the song ended. People on the dance-floor seemed to realize it was the last song of the evening and they stayed and clapped, urging the players to do an encore, but the house-lights came up and recorded music blared from the speakers.

By now Margaret was really drunk. She was struggling with her tongue, trying to tell Neill that she'd been practising chimpanzee noises in an effort to get inside Lucy. She'd watched Jane Goodall programs over and over. Found memories of chimpanzee-like movement in her own limbs, practised chimpanzee expressions in her bathroom mirror. "They come naturally," she said, and demonstrated her imitation of a fear grin. Phillip joined their table again and Neill passed him the drink he'd got for him at last call. Someone else from the museum asked Phillip questions about his music and Margaret tried to listen to his answers while still speaking to Neill and got completely jumbled up.

When the group emerged onto the street, Margaret surprised everyone by suddenly performing a chimpanzee call that began in a soft pant-hoot and evolved into a high-pitched screech. The call had started out as an imitation, sounding very much like a chimpanzee, but somewhere in the middle a note of pain intruded and by the end it had become a scream of anguish. Margaret began to cry. Then she threw up in the gutter. Then she just wanted to lie down and sleep.

TWENTY-FOUR

A bluejay's raucous laugh cascaded into her bedroom window, sounding translucently clear in the quiet of Sunday morning. Her body was completely relaxed under the warmth of the blankets and she thought with pleasure about making a pot of coffee and reading yesterday's newspaper in bed.

Then she noticed she was wearing no pyjamas but a black brassière and matching underpants. Her dress was draped over the banister. Her pantihose were rolled up in a bunch under the covers near her feet. She'd woken during the night because she was too hot and the waistband was uncomfortably tight.

The last thing she remembered seeing were her feet on the tiles of a strange bathroom floor. After that it was as though she were watching a movie with only a dialogue track. She could hear Neill and Phillip talking outside the bar.

"I'll take Margaret home," Phillip said. "It would be my pleasure," he added with good-natured irony. Had she even wiped her mouth after vomiting?

Margaret remembered struggling to make her tongue articulate directions to her house from the back seat of Phillip's car. Then she remembered the engine turning off, a car door opening, closing and then the door near her own feet opening. Phillip asking for her keys in a quiet voice.

Through her nauseated, whirling consciousness, she remembered her grandmother's black beaded evening purse glittering against the white linen tablecloth between the bread plate and her wine glass. She hadn't known where else to put it since it had no strap. Usually she carried keys and money in her pockets or in a large bag that would also accommodate her sketchbook, pencil tin, book and groceries. She didn't remember having the purse at the bar. She sat up while Phillip searched the back seat. He found nothing. She lay back down and mumbled how sorry she was. He left and came back. He'd been able to climb through an open window and unlock her house from the inside.

It took all her willpower to move, to get out of the car and walk up the path. When she sank down finally onto her bed she closed her eyes and thanked Phillip repeatedly. She was aware of wanting to say something more but couldn't focus her brain. He took her shoes off, asked her to sit up so he could help her off with her dress, then drew the covers over her and brushed her hair off her face. It was luxury to be able to sink into unconsciousness knowing she would not have to move again until morning.

Another bluejay called from farther away, a laugh and then a cry. The first answered boisterously right outside her window. She sat up slowly. Her head ached and the lining of her stomach felt raw, but otherwise she was surprised how good she felt.

In the bathroom she examined her face in the mirror. Her cheeks were flushed and pillow creases marked one side of her cheek and mouth. She looked warm and crumpled. She splashed cold water on her face and blinked.

In the kitchen she made toast and weak tea, then went into the studio. The reconstruction's presence dominated the small room. Lucy was complete and robustly muscular except that the flesh around her eyes and nose looked eaten away, her belly was superficially dissected and she had no outer ears.

Margaret had completed the recti muscles that ran vertically along the abdomen but had not yet added the linea alba between the recti muscles. This depression ran from the pubic bone to the cartilege at the lower end of the sternum. It presented several apertures for veins and vessels to pass through, but Margaret was not bothering to recreate any but the largest, which was for the umbilical cord. After birth this hole closed and fused into the puckered scar known as the belly-button.

She made a well for the belly-button with her baby finger, then with a pick formed the small irregular folds and the slightly raised inner bump that came when the last withered piece of cord finally fell off. The belly-button was mysterious—a scar from a time when one's life was not autonomous but bound organically to the mother's body. The umbilical cord was like a phone line, carrying not only blood, oxygen, waste and food, but primal emotional messages. The belly-button was like a phone jack that was no longer functional.

Strange to have been so intimate with her mother's body. And now to have been that intimate with a body that was dead and had left so few traces. Stranger still to have been so intimate physically yet so remote emotionally.

She smoothed the belly-button's rim. She and her father had gone to view her mother's body at the funeral home and she'd been shocked by the make-up. Her mother never wore make-up. The eye-shadow was in tones of beige, burnt orange and brown, the blush also beige, mascara applied lightly, her lips outlined perfectly in a plum-coloured red. It made her mother look gaudy—no longer an attractive, intelligent, somewhat beatific woman of forty-eight. She looked like a doll. Margaret found a kleenex, moistened it with saliva and gently began to wipe the make-up off.

"Leave it be, Margaret. It doesn't make any difference. She's already left the world." His resignation enraged her, she wanted to pummel him and his stupid acceptance. "Her body's still here, for Christ's sakes!" she wanted to scream in his face.

"I don't want to remember her like this," she'd answered instead.

"You won't."

Every time Margaret tried to picture the real face the made-up one rose in her mind like a barrier. Even photographs of her mother couldn't dispel the cosmetic image so that Margaret began to wonder if perhaps something about that doll-like face was authentic and accidentally expressed some aspect of her mother. But she didn't think so.

The phone rang and caused a piercing pain behind her eyes. "Margaret? How are you?" Neill asked, chuckling a little. "That was an impressive chimpanzee call outside the bar. You've been practising."

"Mmmm," she answered non-committally.

"Phillip already phoned this morning to ask about you."

"I bet."

"No. He *was* curious why you might drink so much but for some reason he assumed it was a rare occurrence. I told him I barely knew you. For all I know you get that loaded every night."

Just shut up, she thought but didn't respond.

"He seems quite taken with you," he said.

She felt uncertain about her behaviour the previous night. She didn't regret getting drunk, it had been cathartic, but she would have been happier if Phillip hadn't been there.

"Neill, I don't feel that great right now. What do you want?"

"Really I phoned out of concern. It occurred to me that you might be working too hard. I don't know you very well, I realize, but I know the signs of getting over-involved in your work. As I think I told you, I once had numbers gather together on the pages of a notebook and begin copulating. I've heard voices and I've seen my own body grow scales and claws. When stuff like that begins to happen it's time for a break."

Margaret wanted to know every word Phillip had said about her. And she wanted to know everything

Neill knew about Phillip. Instead they talked about the reconstructions.

Afterward Margaret went out into the backyard. It was sunny and hot. There were dead leaves on the lawn. She looked up and saw they had come from the dogwood tree whose leaves were curled and edged with brown, and she was momentarily disoriented, thinking she must somehow have lost the last weeks of summer. But the leaves on the other trees were still green. It was only the middle of August.

Her sunflowers had opened into large yellow blooms but the seeds were not yet ripe. The large shasta daisies were open; some of their heads were already shaggy and drooping. The black-eyed Susans were just starting. A small zucchini had formed at the base of a large trumpet-shaped orange bloom. Green tomatoes clustered under the leaves of their plants.

A potted hydrangea she'd bought a month ago to plant opposite her rosebush had outgrown its container. The petals on its blooms had wilted and turned inward and some leaves had crumpled and fallen off. She didn't really feel like digging but got the shovel out of the garage anyway.

As she tore at the roots of the grass and caused turmoil among the worms and beetles below, she began to feel as though she were dissecting the earth, that her shovel was a rough scalpel invading a dark, sexual place, tearing open what should be closed, exposing what should be hidden, as though she were probing crudely into a living womb, a womb where an erect penis was still thrusting, seed spurting out.

She had to stop. Let it be. She dropped the shovel on

the grass. The hydrangea could die. It wouldn't matter. She filled the watering can and gave it a long drink, then went round to the front porch. There was an old sofa in the corner which she lay on. Large, plump clouds floated by in the blue sky.

She felt like a giant lens, impersonal, unblinking, watching. Inside she was like an empty room with a strong wind blowing through, the curtains waving wildly. She was no one. Only her senses were real.

A car door opened, then closed. An engine started up. Children shrieked with pleasure in the front yard across the street. A small child started to cry. A bee buzzed near the porch roof, bumping into the wood as though it expected to chance upon the entrance to its hive.

A few days later, the phone rang. She'd been completely absorbed in her work so for a moment she hesitated. It was John. She felt a mixture of irritation and mild curiosity.

A little clay from her fingers stuck to the receiver, then fell to the floor. He sounded nervous. He'd phoned a lawyer and suggested she should too.

"How are you?" he asked warily.

"Working hard... And you?"

"Fine. Working hard too." As she listened she stroked the tendons of Lucy's hand just above the knuckles.

"You're seeing someone?" she asked.

"No. Well, yes. Dating."

"Oh." Not asking if she was.

It seemed ridiculous to have slept in the same bed for years with this man.

"I was a great coward, John. I could have suggested

we see someone for help instead of just clamming up and feeling sorry for myself."

"Don't. Let's just separate the property. It's okay, Margaret." She realized he thought she was trying to reconcile.

"Take care of yourself," she said and hung up abruptly.

An unformed face, roughly cut.

A stone tomb where desire, finding no way out, has died a foetal death. Yet rises again—a white, waxy berry—so unripe, inchoate, deprived of light and oxygen—not blind desire but desire unsighted—waiting in dormancy like a tick or flea until the warmth of something live passes by and wakes it, and it jumps up and embeds itself in the host.

First form the mouth. It must breathe. A doorway from inside to outside. It must kiss.

The lips are full and round and criss-crossed with lines that grow deeper toward the corners of the mouth. The skin would be the colour of nipples, the colour of some parts of the genitals. Nature is so helpful with sex. Touch by number—here and here and here. Kiss-kiss. But these lips are marble—black, white, grey—this skin the colour of stone, these lips the colour of skin, the colour of hair, the colour of chips on the floor.

Closed. Counsel kept. The chisel only forces the lips tighter together. Sealing secrets inside.

Yet the mouth has an ampleness that begs a kiss, a look, a touch. Love could be found in someone's unconscious desire to touch these lips, found in this stone ripening into flesh, in sadness, in the gentle instructions of colour and texture, here and here and here, persuading touch to travel over cold marble.

These lips are ready to speak the desires of an undeveloped heart.

Margaret laid her chisel and mallet down. The face was recessed in the marble, detailed and secret. Margaret planned to leave the rest of the stone rough and uncarved. The mouth was wide though less prognathous than an ape's, more human. The lips were round and firm. They were closed, neither smiling nor pouting, but suggesting desire and sadness, waiting to be touched, or perhaps to speak, stimulating the viewer by action withheld.

Since John called she'd done nothing but work, either on the reconstruction or on her sculpture. She'd spoken with Neill once on the phone to discuss ordering the hair, but the rest of the time she'd left her phone unplugged. She'd finished the body and had only the ears and soft tissue around the eyes and nose to complete before painting the skin.

She flopped into her armchair and looked aimlessly around her study, thinking of kissing. Her eyes fell on the stuffed hummingbird on top of her filing cabinet. It was dusty and looked unprized by its owner, shoved to the back, obscured by piles of paper and a gorilla skull.

She picked it up and blew off the dust. Its translucent wings shuddered and the brilliance of the emerald feathers reappeared. She wanted to kiss Phillip. She wanted to press her lips against his and feel blood flush in from the pressure. She wanted his tongue inside her mouth again, to feel its startling, soft penetration. She wanted her mouth to become an organ of touch, the way it was for a baby. She wanted to reach a state of pure pleasure

and abandonment kissing the small of his back; the concave area between thigh and testicle; the tender underside of his arm; his tight achilles tendon; his clavicle;
and his lips again.

The following Monday she was once more in the dentist's
waiting room. This was her second-to-last appointment
and her teeth were feeling strong and solid. She was so
relaxed now about the needle that she could experience
its sharp jab into the bone consciously, without trying to
block it out. During the drilling she sometimes even
dozed off and Dr. Adin had to rouse her because her jaw
was beginning to close on his hand. The only part of the
process she was still not relaxed for was the initial bite of
the steel clamp on her gums.

The receptionist told her the dentist was running late
because of an emergency. Margaret didn't mind waiting.
Since the banquet, time seemed to pass for her the way
it had when she was a child absorbed in solitary play,
constructing miniature worlds with blocks and dolls and
toy cars. She enjoyed being alone, thinking.

The memory of her mother singing "Chick-a-dee-
dee-dee" flickered across her mind—her happy childhood memory—her mother's voice flying out in the hot
field among the grasshoppers, milkweed and dry, straw-
coloured grass. It was the only time she remembered her
mother sounding happy. Interesting that it should have
been in the voice of another animal.

As Margaret leafed through a magazine, she suddenly
realized she was fooling herself remembering the
moment only as happy. It had been more complex than
that. It had also been painful. Her mother's momentary

happiness had highlighted how unhappy her mother was normally. It confirmed for Margaret that she did not bring her mother joy. She had begun to watch her mother closely for signs of imminent departure. If she misbehaved she panicked afterwards and apologized over and over.

She was also fooling herself seeing it as a moment of connection between mother and daughter. She had been the only one watching. She the one listening, alert to subtle intonations in her mother's voice, she the witness to her mother's ecstatic face. Her mother had not looked at or listened to Margaret. Her mother's gaze had been skyward, her ears attuned to the chickadee and her own voice. Oblivous to her daughter.

And how different was that moment from the time she'd sat in the funeral home staring at her mother's dead body with its impenetrable cosmetic mask? Her mother's unseen witness again.

Suddenly she understood why her father had had her mother's body removed before phoning. Her mother had killed herself.

The realization was instantly familiar. It had been haunting her. She leaned forward and put her face between her knees, as though stricken with abdominal pain. *She had always known.*

The receptionist called her name and the dental assistant led Margaret to an empty room. She attached a paper bib, checked the tools on the tray and left. Dr. Adin came in pulling on a fresh pair of latex gloves.

"How are you Margaret? We're getting close. What are we doing today?" he said looking at the chart. "One big filling in the bottom left molar, then we have a small one in the upper front for next time and that's it. You'll be good as new."

She closed her eyes.

"No sleeping now," he said as he brought the needle round to her mouth.

She worked late every night that week. The photographs of gorilla, human and chimpanzee faces watched her from the wall. In the corner, emerging from its block of marble, her sculpture added to the mingling of ape and human spirits in her studio. She needed nothing else. These companions were enough. She'd worked exceptionally well lately, this evening concentrating perfectly on forming the beautiful shell-like outer ear. She felt calm.

At about three in the morning she sat down in her armchair to rest. She reflected on the importance of small moments in her life and thought how much she liked detail and smallness, and then she began to doze. Her eyelids closed. She forced them open only to have them slide down again. Once more she stood in the ash-covered world.

A moment, listening. A moment of time—before, behind, beyond, below—kings and queens and bombs and guns and countries; civilizations and language and books and science; violins and flutes; bonfires and tents, clothes and tea and bread and curry. Though not before dreams, goosebumps, drums, sticks, stones, splashing, hugs, breast-milk, umbilical cords, ejaculation, cuteness, dying, toothaches, smiles, grins, restlessness, joy. Before loneliness? Not before loneliness.

Not before memory. Or geology. Or footprints: consciousness recorded in earth.

Stop and listen. Listen, listen, *lisssten*... All I see is blue. Listen, listen—what is its voice? Hear what you see. A mountain covered with forest and everywhere blue sky. No, listen. What is the mountain saying? Birds call across its girth at each other. They fly around it as though it were nothing, an old squat ape. A bright yellow-and-black bird with a long tail departs from a tree. No. It tricked you, you're looking. Everything will conspire to keep you from listening. It's not easy. I'm not asking you to do the easy thing. Listen. Listen. Listen.

The sound is of a lens, head tilted back, the eye blue as sky, a huge lens focusing, so cloudless it aches. I hear velocity in the sky; the sound of air rushing to keep up with the earth's surface as it rotates on its axis. This velocity is the sound of time.

I hear time, then, rustle through the leaves of the forest on the mountain, a crowd of minutes rustling, and time tweaks the bird's tail making it fly across my path so I stop listening to watch. The eyes seduce—everyone knows. You desire what you see and are led astray.

But ears are the gateway to angels. You can hear the voice of God, but you perish if you see the divine face unreflected. The light clay between my toes sighs, making a perfect seal against my skin, trapping air pockets. I hear the muck pop as the male walks on. A voice whispers, "Pay attention!" and I stop and turn aside from the path.

Listen, *lisssten*—a snake's voice, or crinkle of dry leaves in autumn wind, or the blazing crackle of heat. A roar fills the air but I don't run away because it comes from inside. It's the sound of blood. Gradually I distinguish specific sounds in the roar. The sound is the same as the velocity I heard in the sky, only more liquid.

Liquid time, dripping, pulsing, squeezing, filtering, the sound of wind rushing in and out; the still moment when quick deals are made; oxygen for carbon dioxide.

A shallow stream fumbling over its bed, a gazelle bends down to drink. Diastole, systole—it expands around my ears like a balloon blowing up, then shrinks suddenly to an empty sac, a bee buzzing, huge—small, huge—small; then the motion jumps into me, and I am huge—small, huge—small, giant—miniature; then the motion spills into the ground which puffs up—sags, puffs up—sags. A rumble in the distance.

The movement slips back inside my skin but this time confines itself to my heart. I hear a cloud releasing raindrops that impact plumply on the ground. I hear other creatures breathing. There are many more than I imagined on these grassy plains at the base of the mountain. The tall wispy sigh of the giraffe, the tiny aspiration of a beetle, a deinothere breathes both through her pink mouth and a long, rattling suction through her trunk. A chalicothere's nails click on the dry mud where she grazes underneath an acacia. Her tail switches back and forth against her flank to worry flies. Guinea hens scritch-scratch on the old river bed. Small hearts inside their eggs beat like flowers. Sweet throbs.

All these companions of the moment. Usually I listen only out of fear, alert for the interruption of sound that accompanies a leopard's stealthy approach. This listening is new to me.

I can't see them.

Who whispered?

The diminutive ape, three foot six, turned back onto her path and continued beside the footprints left by the other one. Perhaps she was followed or accompanied by a smaller one, across the plains of Laetoli, at the foot of Mount Sadiman, just before the volcano showered soft ash over everything, and just before rain transformed the ash into cement that filled and held her footprints and remembered them three and a half million years later in its concrete memory. Listen!

In the dead of night the birds began to call and she was startled awake. Had a leopard climbed the fir tree and disturbed their nests? Where was Lucy? Was she safe?

Then she remembered shaping an earlobe. Slowly she understood there was no Lucy, at least no Lucy that could be harmed by a leopard. Then she knew that there would be no leopard because she lived in a city and because that city was not in Africa. The sun must be rising.

Margaret attached the outer ear to the reconstruction. It attached far back on the head and seemed higher than her own because the crown of Lucy's head was so much lower.

It was enough to be able to listen.

She wet her finger and smoothed the join around the ear. Such a strange thing an ear, a soft spiral dish growing around a small hole in the head, funneling sound-waves from the outside world into the brain. It was a mistake to search for meaning in one's family history, or in ethnicity, or in religion even—only identity could be found there and identity was just a function of the ego's desire to feel safe. It was a mistake to *search* for meaning, period. Ecclesiastes was right. Meaning is the river. Meaning is something you notice when you glance up for a moment from absorbed concentration in your life.

Meaning, like love in the purest sense, can exist only when you don't need it.

Discovering the truth of her mother's death was like discovering something no more meaningful (and no less) than the way the wind scalloped patterns in sand dunes, or the pattern of light on water running over stones—patterns of cause and effect. Her beautiful mother, alone, ready to let go her life-line, so willing to sink quietly, softly into oblivion, drawn to float in a limbo where she hoped the self would not be separate or distinct enough to feel lonely, where if there was consciousness, it would be consciousness of connection, of all things sifting through one another.

Light slowly permeated the branches of the fir tree. The birds verged on cacophony now they sang so loudly. It reminded her of opera, robust and gregarious.

It was enough to listen and watch and feel, to be terrified but curious too. It was enough to work alone, visited by the night sounds of birds and by memories, enough to wander into her kitchen and get something out of the fridge and pick up her tools again and go deeper into her work, excavating and building.

She walked wearily upstairs and slid into bed, overjoyed by the beginning of a glorious day, but content to leave it now and dream. Lucy curled up by her legs, perpendicular to her body, and the pleasure of the warm, soft bed carried them into a deep sleep.

TWENTY-FIVE

U nder the emerald canopy of mature chestnut trees a group of old women, each in her separate world, practised Tai Chi. They moved their limbs slowly, pivoting on one foot and changing direction, their bodies conscious of the space around them and conscious of their own skin. Each movement was existential—raise one leg, rotate one arm—yet each movement was also a testimony that one thing flowed into another, that flesh was an element that melted over time and flowed into all things.

Margaret had woken at six-fifteen after only four hours' sleep eager to work, but there was no cream for her coffee so she'd unplugged the kettle and got dressed.

It was the end of August and the season had already begun to change. The air had lost the hazy thickness of summer and was clear and sparkling. The nights were cold and in the morning a heavy dew soaked the ground. Plants had stopped sprouting new buds and leaves were tinged with yellow. Large adult spiders appeared and spun webs across huge spaces and the webs sparkled with dew until late in the morning.

On her way out of the house that morning Margaret had walked through a web that spanned the eavestrough and the front-porch banister. She couldn't imagine how a spider had transported itself across such a wide horizontal space. Wisps and strands of web trailed from her sweater and hair as she walked across the park where the women were performing their Tai Chi.

She was aware of each tiny hair on her skin. She felt the soft cotton track pants on her thighs, the worn flannel of her shirt across her shoulders. Autumn air puffed under her shirt and cooled her stomach. Dew on the park grass drenched her sandalled feet and made them pleasantly, brilliantly cold.

When she got back home she made a pot of strong coffee and the rich earthy taste saturated her with pleasure. In the studio Lucy only awaited soft tissue to be added under her eyes and her skin to be joined over her nose. In the sketch that had been Margaret's model for Lucy's facial expression, the skin wrinkled around the eyes and over the bridge of the nose, giving the impression of a slight squint. Margaret used a cuticle-shaper to apply the modelling clay. Her fingers worked lightly and quickly to create the fine detail of the small muscles. Once this was done, she lifted a little flap of clay skin that had been folded back and joined it to the bridge of the nose, smoothing a continuity between cheek, brow, temple and nose with her thumbs. She turned the cuticle-shaper upside-down and used the fingernail cleaner to etch in the wrinkles.

Strange process, this returning of flesh to bones it had decayed from millions of years ago. Running film backwards. Maggots furled back into latency, viruses retreating from frothy activity to phlegmatic watchfulness. Yet no quickening, no heart starting up again, no electricity, the flow stagnant, walled inside clay and plastic. This was the only real proof that linear time existed: quickness never returned, though material details might be recreated—the body, the geography, the flora and fauna. Life flowed once, in one direction, it spilt out. Time was a kind of gravity—uni-directional. Once born, minutes poured out of you like spilt blood.

Usually she froze when she thought about time this way. She'd be afraid to act in case nothing happened and she discovered she wasn't alive (she knew how absent-minded she could be). But today the thought of time's velocity excited her.

She ran the cuticle-shaper between her thumb and forefinger to clean off the last bits of clay, then stepped back. The reconstruction was complete and ready to be cast, yet suddenly the face looked lifeless and inert to her. The resurrection had failed. All the king's horses and all the king's men.

It was as though the finished form discouraged the spirit from visiting. While the reconstruction had been incomplete, Lucy's spirit was enticed out to fill in the gaps. Now there was no empty space. The clay crowded the spirit out. The house suddenly seemed empty.

Lucy gazed at her with glassy eyes. A breeze tickled the hairs on Margaret's arm and blew a few pieces of paper toward her across the table. She heard the cover of the mail slot open and shut. She could never resist going and checking the mail, even though there was nothing except bills and junk mail and occasionally a magazine.

A letter addressed by hand and postmarked in Toronto lay on the doormat beside a real estate flyer listing all the homes sold recently in her neighbourhood.

August 24

Dear Margaret,

The chimpanzee call you made the other night expressed such sadness and timelessness. It was primitive and raw. You've been in my thoughts since we met a year ago, but now I must admit I can't stop thinking about you.

I've taken two weeks away from my business to perform in Toronto at a bar that's like a dimly lit cafeteria. The audience is a mix of university students, office workers, artists, plumbers, lawyers, alcoholics—it's a good place to play. Your primate call inspired a new composition, a short version of which I performed last night (Jane's Last Call). I'd like an opportunity to play it for you.

After we met last year I didn't know how to get in touch with you or if I should, but now I've had the good fortune to meet you twice by chance and I don't want to have to depend on a third coincidence. I'd like to see you again soon.

Phillip

The following morning the museum's moulding and casting expert came to her studio and began the work of making a silicon inner mould and a fibreglass mother mould of Margaret's finished reconstruction. On the third day he removed the moulds in sections, bolted the sections together and poured in soft urethane, adding a harder urethane substructure for support. The urethane was tinted a dark brown—the colour Neill had selected as a base skin colour

After the expert left, Margaret added nuance and detail to the new cast of the reconstruction, painting the face, nipples, nails and palms of the hand with a fine paintbrush. By the end of the week she was ready to begin adding fur.

Neill had saved chimpanzee and orangutan fur from his dissections and had dyed the orangutan fur to match the chimpanzee's. She sorted through two cardboard boxes of it, laying out the clumps in order of length and thickness. She decided to start with a place that would likely have been sparsely covered—the sides of the chest under the arms. She sprayed one side with a slow-drying polymer aerosol glue and slowly began laying down long, fine, orangutan fur.

She'd managed to cover one side and part of the trunk before she acknowledged something was beginning to bother her. Though the fur they were using was real, it was also dead. It had no lustre and no roots and it looked like hair on a wig. All the care she'd taken to give the reconstruction a sense of physical immediacy, of vitality and tension, was being deadened by the fur. She phoned Neill.

"Couldn't we just display paintings of them with fur

beside the reconstructions?" Margaret complained. "The hair is so overpowering. It takes over every surface. It obscures all subtleties of the creature's form underneath."

"They are meant to represent our best scientific guess of what afarensis looked like. At the last committee meeting we all agreed it was a very good guess that they had at the least a sparse covering of body hair. It would be irresponsible to suggest hairlessness—"

"I'm not suggesting hairlessness," she interrupted. "I'm suggesting we illustrate the fur in a painting but keep the reconstructions free of hair for purposes of making it easier for people to compare them physically with humans."

"The display is going to include large photographs of the reconstructions in progress, plus a poster-size one of each complete afarensis before fur."

"But it's the presence of the *body*, the sense of a living being that's going to get lost. They're going to look like stuffed monkeys. It doesn't even look like real hair."

"It's more realistic than no hair at all. Look, I'll come over tomorrow morning, just after ten if that's okay, and I'll show you another technique that might produce better results. It involves cutting off half the eye of a needle to make a punching tool and you punch the hair into the reconstruction, one to three strands at a time. It's more time-consuming but it allows much more control of hair density."

"Okay. Ten's fine. See you tomorrow."

She sat and stared at Lucy, trying to visualize what the fur should look like. One problem was the way the fur was lying. Flat. Lucy was supposed to have just heard something that made her stop in her tracks and turn to one side. She would have been alarmed, even if only mildly, and her hair would have stood at least somewhat on end. Neill's technique probably wouldn't help this. What might work? Hairspray? She retrieved a can that she kept in the laundry room for removing ink marks and sprayed a small test area of the fur, then shaped it with a wide-toothed comb.

With such a small area it was too hard to tell, so she sprayed the rest of the hair and pressed it a bit flatter. With a protein spray to give the hair some lustre she thought it would definitely look more alive.

The phone rang.

"Hello, Margaret?"

"Yes."

"This is Phillip." He paused, as though considering carefully what he would say next. "How are you?"

"I'm fine. How are you?" *I could do somersaults in the air.*

"Good. A bit jet-lagged. You got my letter?"

"Yes. Thanks." Her emotions felt too extreme, unstable, not yet founded on reality, so she spoke carefully, monitoring herself.

"Did you ever find your purse? I checked again in the car."

Purse? Her grandmother's evening purse had completely slipped her mind. She'd found a spare house-key which solved the problem of her lost keys, and then she'd forgotten about it. Now she felt a pang at its loss. How long would they keep something like that unclaimed at the bar? Could she still get it back?

"Not yet," she answered, "but I've still got a couple of places to try."

"Could I invite you out to dinner tomorrow night?"

"Yes, that would be great. I'd like that."

"I'll pick you up at six-thirty?"

"Yes. I'll see you then." They said goodbye and she hung up the phone.

Well. Great. She breathed. Well. Being near him for a whole dinner. Hearing his voice from across a table. After a year.

She phoned Neill to get the name of the bar, then looked the number up in the phone book. "Yup, it's here," said a man after going to check. "Kind of sparkly. Keys inside and looks like a lipstick. Yup, it's black."

After Neill left the next morning she started house-cleaning. She hadn't really cleaned, except for the occasional sweep and vacuum, since David, June and Helen had come for dinner over four months ago. She began by throwing things out: clothes she hadn't worn for ten years, magazines, books she'd never reread, paid bills, two ugly brown vinyl chairs. Then she cleared every statue, rock, bone, photograph and piece of china off every windowledge, tabletop and bookcase in every room except the studio.

She carted all the stuff out to the garage. Its shelves were crammed with jars of nails, screws, nuts, wallpaper ends, linoleum ends, pieces of eavestroughing, old paint cans. John had wanted to throw it all away but she'd said no, it would be like throwing out a ship's log. Some of the stuff was from eighty years ago when the house was first built. John claimed she could come up with a rationale for not cleaning anything. If she was going to say that cleaning the garage was erasing history, to be consistent, he said, you shouldn't take a bath or blow your nose or flush the toilet. You should hold on to every trace of every moment you have ever lived.

"I've had to make a few concessions to be a part of this society," she'd answered, because she was in a good mood, and John had laughed and left the garage untouched.

Now she felt differently. She wanted to travel light. She no longer wanted to gather all the evidence of the past around her. She wanted order. Spareness. She wanted to surround herself with light, not matter; with time, not artifacts.

At four-thirty she gave up. She was overwhelmed by how much more there was to be done. She wanted to keep going. She wanted to tear up the stained wall-to-wall carpet, sand and varathane the wood floors; she wanted to paint all the walls, which were grey with dirt and fingerprints, and erase the lighter rectangles where John's paintings had hung. She wanted to throw out the fraying lumpy mustard-coloured couch and make some large inexpensive floor pillows to sit on instead. She felt suddenly extremely impatient with the house's look of drab neglect. She wanted to shake off clutter and dust and useless objects and walk cleanly and clearly through her life. She wanted her house to reflect her inner world, she wanted every colour and every texture and every image to be there because she had chosen it.

She ironed a pair of thick-ribbed black corduroy pants and a loose, flowing white silk shirt. She wore brown suede boots, earrings of dark amber set in tarnished silver and dark-red lipstick. She even painted her toenails a subdued clay pink.

When the doorbell rang she was sitting in her studio

again staring distractedly at Lucy's fur. It was 6:25. He stood on her front porch, the sunset behind him, his blue eyes almost lavender in its intense red shadow, holding a bouquet of autumn flowers—black-eyed Susans, daisies, asters and branches of salal with shrivelled dark-purple berries. In the other hand he carried his saxophone case. He gave her the flowers and kissed her cheek. "From the garden," he said. He followed her to the kitchen and watched her remove dried roses from a vase, rinse it out and put his flowers in.

"Do you like gardening?" she asked. Her eyes travelled self-consciously to her own garden, wondering how it might look to Phillip. She couldn't believe what she saw. Flowerbeds popped up willy-nilly across the lawn, filled with pansies, nasturtiums, daisies, peonies, rhododendrons and lupins. Piles of dirt and grass clumps lay beside empty beds. It looked like some rabid dog had been frantically digging for a bone. She couldn't even remember specifically digging most of the beds, didn't remember planting flowers in them. What had she been doing this summer? *Mary Mary quite contrary, how does your garden grow? With silver bells and cockle shells, and pretty maids all in a row.* Side by side in a graveyard, offering their bodies for compost, helping the garden grow.

"I like the smell of cut grass and oddly enough I like weeding, but I wouldn't say I'm a real gardener. I don't plant many flowers."

The grass between the flowerbeds was a foot high. She'd never even thought about cutting it. "The lawn mower's too big to fit between the flowerbeds," she said.

"You need an electric trimmer." Phillip leaned over

the kitchen table and looked out at the backyard. "It looks like something from *Alice in Wonderland*. What's it going to look like when you're finished?"

Phillip drove an old Ford Fairmont, a sedate-looking, royal-blue, four-door sedan. It was unpretentious and utilitarian and had a dent in the back right fender. He looked old-fashioned behind its wheel, like a farmer driving to Sunday church. It was immaculate inside.

All through dinner she couldn't stop thinking about his feet. She was aware of the weight of his shoes, which were wing-tipped brogues. She liked their sturdiness and civility, a good shoe for a weekend walk on a country path. And she thought of the foot inside them, the achilles tendon, the ropy calf muscles, his hard knees under the beige corduroy pants, the quadriceps. He shifted position in his chair and his foot bumped hers under the table and she was momentarily unable to concentrate on what he was saying. Throughout the meal she always knew where both his feet were.

When they got back to her house, she invited him in for a drink. She poured them a couple of scotches in the kitchen while he went through her records. He chose *The Swan of Tuenola* by Sibelius, with David Oistrakh on violin, and Joni Mitchell's *Blue*, which he put first on the turntable.

She set his drink on the floor beside him and sat down sideways on the awful mustard-coloured sofa. They listened to the song without talking.

Margaret looked out the living-room window at the streetlamp, at raindrops falling through its light. Something felt deeply familiar to her watching the rain fall against the darkness. It could've been anything falling—snow, flakes of ash, dust—minute after minute after minute. She had a sense of being watched, a sense of imminent pleasure, and of sadness. One day in the past it had been ash that was falling from the sky and turning sunlight to a shrouded dark red. Footprints of passersby—guinea hens, prehistoric elephants, Lucy— had been made, and then it had been rain that fell. One evening in the past it had been snow falling, and Margaret's tracks on fresh snow made a path to her parents' house and were filled again with more snow before she left. Now rain was falling outside her house and Phillip was in the house, looking at her with pleasure and curiosity. The past and present seemed at that moment to exist simultaneously, to both be real and present, and she felt relieved.

The needle rose and swung back onto its cradle. Phillip got his saxophone case and opened it beside her on the sofa. His sweater, dampened by rain, smelled of sheep. He assembled the instrument and brought the reed to his lips. The first live notes inside the small room were hair-raisingly loud and alive—the sound was of a completely different order from that made by the record-player. The piece was a wild exuberant lament.

Margaret took off her coat and hung it up on one of the hangers provided for patients in the dentist's waiting room. It was a plaid coat from the fifties. The fabric was off-white, woven with mustard yellow and olive-green threads, and the collar and pockets were trimmed with light-brown suede. It had been her grandmother's country coat and Margaret was fond of it even though the wool was very worn on the edges. It was only nine o'clock in the morning yet the waiting room was already occupied by another man and woman, which meant a wait of at least half an hour.

She sat down and riffled through the magazines on the table beside her chair. An orangutan caught her eye on one of the covers. She picked up the magazine and leafed through looking for the article while congratulating herself again on how much better her reconstruction was looking. Using both the new technique and the hairspray, the fur now had texture and electricity and the reconstruction had regained some of its vitality and kinesthetic presence.

The receptionist called out, "Mr. Shertock," and a muscular man in his forties stood up, shoulders hunched, head down, and walked like a condemned man into the dentist's room.

She found the title page of the orangutan article accompanied by a photograph of an adult male orangutan high up in the trees. The article described how solitary these "men of the forest" were, and how it could be years before a male and a female even encountered one another. How different from the line-up of suitors a sexually active female chimpanzee attracted every time she went into estrus. Margaret remembered the sudden pangs of envy that scene had inspired in her and her despair of ever being desired that much by a man. It seemed so long ago that John had lived in the house, sat behind his newspaper, never touching, never asking about her, so long ago since she realized how lonely and unwanted she was.

Skin. Shadow changing density, adapting itself unpossessively to the contours of flesh, saturating the concave surfaces with beautiful soft penetrable blackness and lighting convex surfaces—quadriceps, biceps, buttocks. Thinking about that skin was like swooning into warm darkness. The dark coin of areola and in the coin's centre a nipple—its skin so tender and sensitive, yet erect and thrust outward into a world of rough textures. She had put her mouth around it. Too intimate to think about.

His eyes changed as they moved from light to shadow —the pale blue of a winter morning to the indigo of twilight. They twinkled above her with such warmth and delight she felt like a bouncing baby girl, gurgling and smiling, waving chubby legs and arms, lovable and perfectly content. She laughed up at him and he asked her why. "I feel like a baby," she said.

"How so?"

"Happy."

They created an ocean of time and slipped inside. She was sometimes a baby, sometimes a goddess and sometimes Lucy. She became volcanic, erupting molten-red and orange, swollen with blood; and then she was cool and quiet, moving to and fro in an ocean current, feeling her history back to single-celled life in tidepools.

When she curled herself around him and enveloped his penis in her mouth, she was saturated with peace and calm, as though she were transporting them both in a clear acrylic spaceship into the large quiet deep open spaces of the universe, stars around them. *The Owl and the Pussycat went to sea in a beautiful pea-green boat.* His hand stroked her hair. He rubbed the nape of her neck with his thumb.

Afterwards she couldn't sleep. Her head rested on his

inner thigh and her back curved against his belly. He held her ankle lightly in his sleep. The moon shone onto the bedcovers. She pulled a sheet over her legs and feet. The rain had stopped. She could see the clouds being broken up by wind and pushed quickly away.

Late the next morning she woke, her head still on Phillip's thigh, the end of a dream spilling over into wakefulness.

An old chimpanzee crouched beside a river peering at her reflection in an eddy caused by the branch of an uprooted tree. She chattered and exclaimed to herself and rocked back and forth on her heels, looking at the pool like someone looking out over an open landscape at sunset. An old woman walked over to the creature, sat down and peered curiously into the pool too. Through the slight blur of age their eyes met in the water's reflection and for a moment, the two females considered one another in their old age, life gazing upon life, vision upon vision, a circle of screams and warmth, comfort and cold, of grass and termites and pomegranates, mud and warm rain, snakes, fire and shadows, whispers and roars and teeth and bones, nuzzling, wandering, exclamations and clouds, stars, water, dinosaurs and airplanes, lions and testicles and nipples, blood, tickling, candles.

Two forms curl together, old and dissolving, the black fur worn away and the soft, wrinkled skin, the empty uteruses and breasts, complete in their emptiness, curling deeper and deeper into one another.

The other woman in the waiting room went over to the receptionist's desk and asked how much longer. The receptionist glanced at her appointment book. "Another five minutes. It's an extraction and it's a tricky one, but it shouldn't be long now."

Margaret turned the page of the magazine to a photograph of Professor Birute Galdikas holding hands with a young orangutan. They seemed like companions, the woman and the young ape, as though they were enjoying each other's company as they walked through a camp in Borneo.

Phillip had woken shortly after Margaret and they lay together and he stroked her ankle while she told him about the dream. Then she stretched, reaching her arms over her head and pointing her toes. Something about lying on a bed with no covers—the covers were crumpled on the floor at the end of the bed—made her feel both safe and free, as though she were in a field on a warm sunny day with nothing but time on her hands and pleasure ahead. She felt like scampering around, jumping up and down, hooting, banging sticks against trees, wrestling. Phillip kissed the small of her back. She felt as though the part of her that overlapped with Lucy, the primate part of her, was fully alive at last. She felt like flexing her muscles and bouncing off the walls. She felt strong and quick.

She stretched again and rubbed the length of her body against Phillip. She got on her hands and knees and he held her haunches and pushed inside her and she rocked back against him, coiled like a lioness, galloping, springing across wide open spaces, her back glistening with perspiration, panting and crying out, faster, faster, flexing her muscles to their limit, running herself as fast and hard as she could, shaken by wave after wave of desire and pleasure.

She turned unconsciously to a photograph of a baby orangutan following Professor Galdikas. Since she'd remembered her dream the other morning, she had not felt Lucy as a separate presence floating inside her body any more. Some alchemical process had occurred. It felt as though the molecules forming her body had come unglued into separate atoms and then recombined with Lucy's atoms.

A few minutes later she was settling back into the comfortable curve of the dentist's chair. The other woman was in the adjacent office. The assistant clipped a paper bib around Margaret's neck, adjusted the chair then left. She'd forgotten to bring the magazine in with her so she looked out the window for distraction. A young man, tall and slim, leaned against one of the posts of the bus shelter. He wore a navy T-shirt that was way too big for him and made his neck and arms look skinny and vulnerable. He picked up a stone and skipped it down the sidewalk. It bounced twice then disappeared into someone's lawn.

Dr. Adin strode into the room and greeted her with his usual enthusiasm. He picked up her chart, glanced at it and tossed it on the counter.

"Open." He put pressure on her upper left gum with his finger, then jabbed it with the needle. "One smallish filling here, crown the bottom molar—it arrived yesterday—and you're good as new. Close. I'll come back when you're frozen." He waved at the doorway.

The young man at the bus stop reminded her of a photograph in one of her books about human evolution—a thin, Ethiopian man standing on a hillside of powdery, slightly reddish dust, digging with a garden spade. The man was digging in Afar, the region in

Ethiopia where Lucy was found.

Afar. She heard the English words echoed in the Ethiopian name for the first time. Afar. A far and wrinkled land, deeply furrowed, with naked ridges where bones are laid bare. Another order of geography.

The perfect spacial expression of Ecclesiastes, Genesis—from dust you were made, to dust you shall return. Here. Now. Shoes planted deep in red dust on the side of a red hill. The air is so dry your sweat evaporates before it beads. At the same time, the same moment, you stand simultaneously in the past, by the cool bank of a shallow river, grass to your shoulders, mud between your toes. Listening... Listening to birds, listening for the *swish-swish* of a cat's tail...for the whisper of its panting.

Afar. Where your feet, planted in red dust, are synchronously in the mud of a river bank, where being present means being in the future looking back at a shard of the self, and being in the past means glimpsing that future ghost shifting its weight from one foot to the other, tired of standing on a hill in the hot sun.

A geography where past and present conflate, where the self standing in dust can gaze clearly down time to a distant present. A place where your ego does not cut the view short, like a guillotine.

Dr. Adin came back into the room carrying a small box. "Are you frozen?" She nodded. He tilted the chair back. "Open. You won't need freezing for the crown. Just a little discomfort around the gums. I'll do it first." He popped the temporary crown off.

"How've you been keeping?" he inquired as he sprayed the area where the new crown would go. Was he expecting her to gurgle an answer? Did he expect her to remember the question and answer when he was finished? She was beginning to suspect that he enjoyed asking questions but didn't have the patience to endure answers.

The assistant held the saliva suction in place as he turned and got the new crown out of its box. Margaret's tongue darted tentatively toward the peg that the original tooth had been filed down to.

"Fine," she slurred.

"Gooood," he said slowly as he concentrated on fitting the crown over the peg. He eased it under the gum line. This area was quite tender and she winced whenever it pinched the inflamed surface. *One minute*, she told herself. *You can survive one minute of pain.*

When he was finished Dr. Adin praised his work softly, like a gardener admiring newly planted flowerbeds. He handed Margaret a tiny round mouth mirror on a long curved handle so she too could admire the new crown. Her teeth felt so strong now it seemed they might outlive the rest of her. Perhaps they were too strong. Perhaps they'd go on chewing long after the rest of her body had decomposed. Dr. Adin's hand inside her mouth, tightening the clamp for the rubber dam, her teeth, deciding they don't need him any more, they've had enough discomfort, coming down on his knuckles. They drag her out of her seat, past the receptionist, past the coat closet, out into the world. The walking jaw.

"How's the reconstruction progressing?"

"Almost finished. I'm sticking in the last of the fur. It has to be ready for delivery next week."

"I'm looking forward to seeing it. When's the opening?"

"October first."

Dr. Adin motioned for her to open again. He pushed the rubber dam further down over her tooth, probed the tooth with a pick, then readied the drill.

"Hmmm. What's next for you?" he asked, peering down at her through his glasses. His gaze moved to inside her mouth and he started to drill. Margaret gripped the chair to keep from laughing out loud. This was torture.

The sun passed below the horizon and the sky deepened to purply blue, the same hue as the blooms on the hydrangea. The weather over the past couple of days had been a last pulse of summer, hot and sunny and bright, warm enough for plants to grow, but the plants remembered the cool snap at night and neither grew nor withered. Margaret stared down at her ragged, patchwork garden from the bedroom window. She was restless. She'd finished the reconstruction that afternoon. She went back downstairs to her studio to stare at it again.

Tomorrow the museum's truck would pick up everything belonging to the museum. She began packing the various bones into the crates they'd arrived in and decided to leave the replica fossils of the Lucy skeleton until last.

She was afraid of losing Lucy. She feared the return of the anxiety that had paralysed her in the morning before Lucy had arrived. She feared time yawning out in front of her like a black hole intersected only by her own death, and she feared being thrown back on herself—slam! wind knocked out, legs crumpling. She feared the loss of this interested creature and she feared the loss of her own past slipping away into the dark folds of a curtain on an empty stage. Alone in her house again, dreaming, a strange menacing voice pretending to offer help, keeping his own agenda concealed.

The sun pulled the last rays of light down with it under the earth and she could see objects only in silhouette—Lucy's profile, leaning forward, facing an unknown world, an unknown life, armed only with a simple intention to live.

Margaret turned on the lights and continued packing. For Lucy the unknown could metamorphose into a leopard, two daggerlike canines might penetrate her watchful tender brain. She might die in terror. That was the deal. Live with fear and pain and danger or don't live. No alternative.

Margaret's mother had accepted these terms. And her mother had made a commitment. There was no clutching, no frantic casting about; just a gentle, dignified opening of the fingers, a ceasing to hold the life-line, a sweet drifting out—no regrets—not even for those she left behind.

Margaret began crying. She'd been so unwilling. She had kicked and screamed, complained, threatened, moaned, fled—she had married her husband for comfort and when marriage proved just as frightening and strange as the rest of life, she'd sought comfort in sleep. What a coward. She'd spent her whole adult life lacking commitment—vacillating—she'd cast about frantically, ingloriously, shamelessly, looking for another way, another option. She had chosen comfort every time, and every time she had not been comforted.

The intensity and excitement of the last few days suddenly drained from her and she felt very tired. She looked at her watch, it was five after one, so she went upstairs and got her pillow and her sheet and carried them back down into her studio. She spread the sheet on the floor under the window. She took another sheet from the linen closet and floated it down beside the first. On this she lay the fossils of Lucy's skeleton, one by one, in their proper relationship. Then she lay down beside them and slept.

The moon shone through the low branches of a fir tree onto the fragmentary skeleton assembled beside the warm fleshy body of a woman, curled loosely in a foetal position, her hair spread on the pillow, her legs covered by white cotton, her side rising and falling with each breath.

TWENTY-SIX

S he is floating over clear black water in a white row-boat big enough only for one. The water is perfectly calm. Morning sunlight penetrates the mist and illuminates tiny specks under the water and makes them sparkle. She is aware of the vast dark space below her. She is in a fjord. Beside her are steep slate-coloured cliffs. Birch trees grow at the top in sunlight. Behind her is a great field of tall yellow grass. She is nine months pregnant, which seems miraculous and makes her deeply happy. The boat is very low in the water.

About fifteen feet in front a spout erupts from the sea and showers her with a gentle mist. It's a killer whale's spout. She never sees the whale but she feels its presence all around her. She senses it came to visit her. When it leaves she feels alone in this beautiful place, but connected to everything from her small boat.

TWENTY-SEVEN

Margaret entered the new Hall of Human Origins alone. A well-dressed crowd sipped wine and conversed while young women in white shirts and black skirts or trousers offered trays of hors d'oeuvres and paper napkins.

Frank and Neill stood together across the hall, and as she made her way toward them she caught a glimpse of Lucy between people's hips. She looked so small. More like a monkey than an ape. And it was this small-ness more than her furriness that made her look animal and feral.

The crowd closed in again and Margaret joined Frank and Neill, who were talking to a woman Margaret recognized from the fund-raising banquet. Neill seemed unusually happy and animated as he spoke.

"The mating system would not have been monoga-mous. There's too big a size difference between the sexes.

Males would probably have competed among themselves for access to females. I didn't want the male afarensis to look like he was in the middle of a confrontation with another male, yet I wanted some menace or defensiveness, some reference to the origins of our own territoriality and aggression. That's why the eyes are low and hooded, sizing the viewer up, ready to challenge. Primate meets primate."

"Margaret!" Frank said, interrupting Neill. "Can I buy you a glass of wine? White or red?"

"Red, thanks."

"Margaret! Hello!" Neill exclaimed and kissed her cheek. "Excuse me, Mrs. Cooper-Smith, this is my colleague Margaret Fisher, creator of the female Australopithecus afarensis. Margaret, Ralph Pettigrew, the world-renowned paleoanthropologist, told Frank he thinks our reconstructions are quite credible. He has one small argument with the noses, but that's all. *That's* an incredible achievement, let me tell you. He's an extremely critical, antagonistic guy."

Frank handed her a glass of wine. "Margaret, excellent work! I know I've already told you this but I love the way you built Lucy. She looks so primitive and robust and yet at the same time thoughtful and vulnerable. She is very expressive. And I think you captured the aspect of hesitation perfectly!"

He clapped his hands and rubbed them together. She felt a wave of affection for the two men and their bounding enthusiasm, their proud satisfaction at the Laetoli display and their inclusion of her in their circle of satisfaction. They were like proud parents at their off-spring's coming-out party.

Frank patted her on the back and left to greet someone just entering the hall. The woman from the fund-raising banquet asked Neill another question and Margaret excused herself on the pretext of getting some food. She picked out a large strawberry and went over to the display.

She thought she'd envisioned Lucy in the context of the display all along as she'd worked, but the truth was she hadn't. For example, she was shocked at how huge the male afarensis looked next to Lucy. A fourteen-inch difference in height hadn't seemed really that significant, but, when coupled with the huge difference in body mass and the male's massive strength, Lucy looked like a timid furry child in comparison.

And the gaze Margaret had planned to converge at the average person's eye-level three feet away was converging instead just above their belly-buttons. Only by crouching down could the small dark face be seen and the creature's benevolently framed question—who are you?—recognized.

Margaret had only experienced Lucy on the foot-high stand she'd built her on. Down from this pedestal, feet anchored to a concrete set of footprints, she seemed trapped in a tightly parenthesized moment. Everyone but Lucy could see where her next steps would lead, and everyone but she knew she would die and her whole species would die. And yet there she stood, hesitating, slightly apprehensive, as though she might actually choose to turn away from her path. The irony of the scene made Margaret feel sad for Lucy, but she hoped it lent the reconstruction a certain humanness, a destiny humans could identify with, however uncomfortably. Who doesn't die? What species doesn't become extinct?

The only question is what lies between now and death, now and extinction. The present and the present and the present.

Margaret sat down on a brand-new thick black vinyl banquette across from the display. The crowd blocked her view, but occasionally it cleared and she could see some part of the display as though through a short, blunt telescope.

Today she'd done some more of the final sanding on her sculpture. A series of sculptures was beginning to fill her body like earth—they had pressure, weight and volume inside her. They looked like death-masks, watching the world not so much from the grave as from a different point in time/space. They were a convergence of souls, animal and human, wandering into her studio, where she anchored them in stone for as long as the stone might last before it crumbled back into the earth. They were like dream watchmen, solemn, angelic, silent.

The next sculpture would be two pieces of stone facing each other: on the right a human cheek and ear and on the left the cheek and ear of Australopithecus afarensis. In both just the ear would be sculpted in detail, the surrounding flesh and hair would be left rough and textured and undefined. The ears would emerge from the stone the way bodies emerge from the earth and melt back into it, the way species emerge from a sea of time and melt back. The ears would be instruments tuned to the exquisitely chaotic singing of angels, tuned to the seesawing absence/presence of God.

"Hey Margaret, you look great!" Helen stepped forward from the crowd, smiling broadly. David was with her. They sat down on either side of her.

"June had to work today," David said apologetically. "She's going to try to make it if she finishes before five. Otherwise she'll meet us at the restaurant later."

"We were looking for you. What a magnificent job you've done. Lucy is wonderful. So poignant and intense. So ape, and yet so human. Very powerful. Congratulations!"

"They seem very realistic," added David with more measured praise.

"We've been circulating and eavesdropping for you. People are amazed to be descended from them. Appalled, excited, encouraged. They're not at all what anyone expected. Where did you get those pants, by the way? They're new, aren't they? They're fabulous!"

Margaret found the way Helen moved so abruptly and unselfconsciously between completely unrelated subjects endearing.

"Yes they are. They're Jaeger. They're really comfortable."

"Who cares about comfortable? You're such a prude sometimes. They're sexy and elegant! And they suit you."

They were the first item of clothing Margaret had ever found that fit her properly. They hung beautifully. The fabric was a soft tawny gabardine, and they reminded her a little of men's pants, except they were more flowing. She'd also bought a plain pale-pink jersey T-shirt and brown lace-up shoes.

She'd bought the pants without hesitation and without trying anything else on to compare. The store was an expensive one, and she'd felt embarrassed and underdressed walking in the front doors, but the saleswoman had been very gracious and within ten minutes had

suggested the plain T-shirt and the shoes, had sum-
moned the store's seamstress to pin up the pants and
rung up Margaret's bill. She'd left the store feeling deci-
sive and very satisfied. She would be able to attend the
opening without worrying that a safety-pin might be
showing, a stain might be noticeable in too bright a
light, without having to cover major flaws with a
sweater, or drape a scarf strategically to hide a missing
button, or pull a shirt out to cover the undone button
of a too-tight waistband. She wouldn't have to conceal
anything.

Dr. Adin appeared in front of the banquette. He had
brought his wife and two daughters. All three were tall
and slender and doe-like, with long straight brown hair
and large brown eyes. The dentist turned toward his
family, beaming with pride and joy, and ushered them
forward as though he needed to help them overcome a
slight shyness.

"The girls are absolutely fascinated," he said.
"Veronica is studying evolution this year in science class,
aren't you, dear?" Veronica, the older one, nodded.
"She's an excellent student. Not to boast. They both are.
Though Jessica is better in the humanities and Veronica's
strength is in sciences. Margaret did the smaller one, the
female," Dr. Adin told his wife.

"She is very beautiful," said Mrs. Adin with a rich
Spanish accent. She spoke, in contrast to her husband,
without excitement but with a measured dignity. She
reminded Margaret somehow of her mother, or rather of
how Margaret imagined her mother had been as a young
woman—a melancholy patience, a sad grace. She caused
Margaret to yearn suddenly to speak with her mother.

Her father had phoned her last week. "Has it arrived?" he'd asked out of the blue. "I sent it by courier to arrive exactly today. Did you get it yet?"

Nothing had arrived.

"It's from your mother. She wanted you to have it on the day you turned 31 years and 256 days old. That was her age the day you were born. Call me when it arrives, otherwise I'll put a trace on it." He paused. "I waited this long to send it. After sixteen years of counting I want it to arrive on the right day."

The parcel had arrived late that afternoon. A shoe box, Bally, Naturalizer, tied with string and sealed with purple sealing wax. Beige pump, size nine. That box, evidence of a day on which her mother had bought herself a new pair of shoes, a mundane act, an act presuming life, presuming the small routine moment of putting shoes on in the morning, filled Margaret with a fresh sense of loss. She thought of her mother tying the string around the shoe box. She would have known then that she was doing each thing for the last time, God bless me at this moment when for the last time—the last time—I tie a piece of string, I write, I sigh, I think of my daughter…I breathe…

Margaret broke the seal, cut the string and opened the lid. A dry musty smell floated up. Cotton balls were packed around several objects wrapped in yellowed tissue paper. An envelope was tucked in the side. She removed the envelope first, thinking it might be a letter. It was unsealed and the edge of the flap was curled and brittle. Inside, two locks of light-brown baby hair nestled beside a tiny square sealed envelope. She tore it open and inside were five child's milk teeth. *They must be mine*, she thought.

Gently she shook the tiny teeth out onto the kitchen table. Artifacts. From when she was a baby. You were a child once. You, sitting now gazing down at parts of yourself in the same way you might look at a museum piece, feeling the same awe as for a millions-of-years-old fossil. Hair and teeth from a child you don't remember being, except for memory fragments, and even those could be imaginary. Your mother remembered you, though.

Remember you were a child, you were my child, I cherished your fine hair and your small teeth. Remember your small self, gaze with wonder on these relics of your smallness, your babyness, a time before measurement, when love flowed like a river, like air.

Eyes, sparkling, warm, fierce, looking down at her, and Margaret round and shiny, bubbling over—it occurred to her now that she must have been remembering her mother looking down at her in her crib, Phillip must have drawn that memory out. How could Phillip look at her with as much love as a mother for a newborn baby? Did he recognize her, the part of her that was there when she was a baby?

She looked up for him near the entrance. She was looking forward to seeing him at a distance, across the hall, to watching him without his knowledge. Then he would touch her shoulder, kiss her, stand beside her.

The adults had been chatting and the girls had whispered together, but now everyone seemed to have run out of things to say. Dr. Adin announced that he and his family should look at the other exhibits since they had to leave soon. David and Helen seemed to realize Margaret was preoccupied and said they'd see her later at dinner.

In one corner of the shoe box coiled in tissue paper she found a string of cultured pearls whose silver clasp was set with tiny diamonds. There was also an old primary school exercise book rolled up and held with an elastic band. In it her mother's cramped and scratchy hand chronicled a six-page account of her life story. She wrote dispassionately, with no comment on the emotional colour or value of each event, but in a separate postscript she'd written: "All my adult life I have suffered a paralysing terror. It was there in the morning before I opened my eyes and there every night as, with relief, I went to sleep. I steeled myself to get through each minute of my life. I am so tired. I am praying that your life will be good. The only difficult thing, Margaret, is leaving you alone."

The last item in the shoe box was a framed black-and-white photograph. The frame was painted a tarnished silver colour and carved with small flowers and ribbons. The glass inside had shattered in long radiating pieces, as though its centre had been struck by a stone.

Margaret carefully removed the shards of glass. The photograph was of her mother as a young woman sitting with Margaret's grandmother in a field of tall grass and wild daisies. The photograph was slightly overexposed so the daisies were luminescent and possessed the slight blur of motion, making them look like white butterflies. Margaret's grandmother looks straight out from the picture and her face is also luminescent. Her matronly body with its generous bosom leans back against a rock. She looks comfortable and at home in the grass. Margaret's mother sits nearby but at an angle, gazing into a distance the photograph is not able to include. Her back is to the sun and her face therefore is more shadowy. Her posture is alert, poised, her head held high; her tall slender body sits lightly among the grass, ready to spring up and run at the first sound. Her pale bare feet look warm, uncalloused and clean. A blur in the top right-hand corner of the photograph is probably a bird.

A young woman came by and offered Margaret a platter of vegetables and dip. She took a floret of cauliflower but avoided the dip, which was pink and shiny. She loved the colour of cauliflower—its undertone of light green, its rich but delicate opaqueness, its antique quality.

The body transcends identity yet the body is not impersonal. The words just floated into her head and sounded as though they meant something. They were associated with Lucy, an awareness she hadn't yet lost. They meant that people were desperate to pry their identities away from their bodies because bodies were perishable. They sought, without dignity, to identify only with the parts of themselves they believed could transcend the body when it started to decay and tumble with maggots—the spirit, soul, mind. Abandoning ship. These captains were not going down with their vessels. The experience of the body was disposable, it was to be used, punished, denied. *But think of memories. Think of dreams. Think of childhood.* The sense of embodiment.

The arrival of her mother's gift had acted like a tiny bolt at the top of a door being drawn back. She saw with perfect clarity how her mother's desire to die had created a black hole in the centre of Margaret's being, even retroactively. In the tiny powerful egocentric frame of her child's understanding she'd always believed that her mother wanted to leave her.

Now she knew that wasn't exactly true. Her mother had wanted to leave, yes, but she hadn't wanted to leave Margaret. In fact the opposite was true. The only reason her mother had lived another seventeen years and denied herself the relief of dying was to stay with Margaret until she grew up. She had taken her daughter to the park, to the library, she had cooked dinner and bought her clothes. She had made a great effort to reach out of her darkness and give her daughter a normal life. Acts that might not be signs of special love in other mothers were in hers.

*Chick-a-dee-dee-dee...chick-a-dee-dee-dee...*a trembling bruised hypnotic soprano trying to approximate the cheery familiar friendliness of a chickadee's song— her mother trying to keep her demons at bay and give her child a normal, light-hearted moment.

It was enough. More than enough. Margaret started to cry. She wanted to tell her mother how grateful she was.

She walked over to a tall oblong window and looked outside so no one would see her wiping her eyes on her sleeve. Outside grey mist hung around the branches of a huge chestnut tree. The tree was old, and she traced the intricate pattern of its branches with her eyes until they became familiar in the way certain objects in her childhood had been—the bathroom tiling, an oriental carpet, the pattern on their dinnerware.

Eventually she stopped crying. She needed to blow her nose and started toward the food table for a paper napkin when she saw Phillip standing by the entrance. She thought he was so handsome. Electric. She took a deep breath and smiled. It was his self-possession that most thrilled her, that made her think of his body's presence in the room as charged, super-conscious, no, perhaps super-unconscious of itself, involuntarily aware of its own flexed muscles, taut tendons. His was the opposite of a dead body. He was charged with a coiled but indolent vitality. And he was looking for her.

She woke. First light touched the hem of the sky. Birds were in full song. Raucous hosanna. *All I know about history*, she thought, vaguely remembering a dream then forgetting it. Phillip lay beside her, sleeping. She got up and went downstairs. She was wide awake, excited and happy. She got a piece of leftover pizza and went outside to see the sunrise. Her feet were still hot from sleep and the cold wet grass shocked them. She hoped in the back of her mind that all the worms were tucked away in their holes and not lying on the ground indistinguishable to her feet from the cold grass. There among the flowerbeds and mounds of earth, she wondered what she'd been looking for under the tangled web of lawn and weeds.

Had she been doing some kind of backyard autopsy? What strange bones had she hoped to unearth, what foetal self, cracked open like the husk of a seed, unfurling, extending toward light and the faintest promise of warmth? She had dug in the earth like someone tunneling into her own womb to search out an unborn voice, encountering death at every turn and swallowing it like a worm, burrowing deeper, deeper, past death into history, into the hidden history of her own body. And at the end of her lightless odyssey through tunnels sodden with rot and growth, seeds and bones, she'd waited to be redeemed under her own skin. Redeemed by what? By insight, there in her backyard and there in the shadowy sockets of a primitive skull, and there in the mottled flesh of stone. She had found not who she was, but something she wasn't looking for.

Margaret laughed out loud in her nightgown and bare feet in the dewy autumn air and her laugh made her think of Sarah, from Genesis, who laughed when God told her that the withered sacks of her aged breasts would suckle new life, would be the fountains of life for generations to come. She who had been barren all her youth. Why should she laugh? After all, what did she know about the mysteries of the world? *Though I dig forever, I cannot uncover the secrets whispering in my own skull, I will never see my own bones.* God shouldn't have been angry with Sarah. Who wouldn't laugh? There was joy in her disbelief, there was reverence in her laughter.

Margaret remembered the smell of earth freshly broken open. She remembered the ache in her hamstrings from crouching, echoing the posture of an ape collecting termites or nomads watching the sunset from a tent doorway. She remembered the various smells of earth: in the morning, in the heat of the afternoon, different again in the evening, each different in each season, each eliciting a sense of *déjà vu.*

She had dug and dug and dug and found beneath the earth's surface—the past, the future, a dark, burrowing present. She was ready—not that she wasn't afraid because she was—but her situation was no longer that of a bird caught in a snake's gaze. She could move now. She could embrace a man—Phillip—knowing he was not her salvation and love him knowing she could not save him either, knowing she was ignorant of love, knowing only one thing. Love required her to loosen her grip on the river's bank, required the discipline to pry her own fingers loose, one by one, and float in a stream of listening, relinquishing all illusion of familiarity, all false promises of safety and comfort.

Listen, listen! A hallelujah to the lives of minutiae, to the tiny osmosis of one-celled creatures, to waving cilia, to the penetration of a fat cell by a thin hungry one wriggling furiously to get in. Listen to a story, or rather myriad stories waltzing through the bodies of creatures alive and dead, stories tumbling across her synapses, whose narratives gliding through the lives of microorganisms like a river running over coloured pebbles, tell all of the unique pleasure of wearing a new hat, the waxy thrust of spring from a subterranean bulb, a glance between a woman and man who have not yet made love.

Who are you?

I float in and out of everything. I am a story telling itself anew every day and I am a familiar old story, "tell me again, mom. I'm not sleepy yet." Oblique, rich, shifting, smoke wending its way upward in a cloud of dancing stories and discrete moments—an exuberant decadent waltz of dust with dust—an explosive spinning heady wedding of dust to consciousness.

The sun came over her neighbour's fence and illuminated her garden.